River Cruise Undercover

A Romantic Travel Adventure

Anna Leigh

Copyright © 2019 Thomas Weaver LLC

All rights reserved.

ISBN: 1-7321991-5-9
ISBN-13: 978-1-7321991-5-6

DEDICATION

For Barbara, who always believed, provided her love and support, and so much more.

This book is a work of fiction. Names, characters, places, and incidents are the product of the author's imagination or are used fictitiously. Any resemblance to actual events, or persons, living or dead is coincidental and unintended.

All rights reserved. The scanning, uploading, reproducing, and transmission or distribution of this work without permission is a theft of the author's intellectual property. Permission for use (other than review) may be obtained from Thomas Weaver LLC at TWeaver2008@aol.com

ACKNOWLEDGMENTS

No book can be completed without the help of many others, usually too numerous to mention all by name. Here are a few, and forgive me if I have excluded someone – I would write someone important, but you are all important to me.

First, my family, without who's encouragement, this would have not been completed. Especially my mom, who always believed. Then, to the group of reviewers who provide valuable insight and impetus for changing this work in ways to make it better, and to Gundi Gabrielle and the SassyZenGirl network for their assistance and helping me to accomplish my goals.

Finally, my gratitude and debt to the reviewer of this work, Jessica Snyder, who not only offered great insights and ideas to make this a better work, but also provided encouragement and praise.

Cover by Lizaa

Anna Leigh

One

The Eurostar train slowed, and Eve Belot opened her eyes to look out the window of the coach as it pulled into the shaded track between gray nineteenth-century buildings at Gare du Nord in Paris. Though the trip from London was only two hours, the constant travel and work this week was exhausting. The next few days in Paris would give her the opportunity to unpack and rest even as she continued to scout couture and ready-to-wear fashions around the city.

She tucked the pencil sketches she'd been reviewing into her camel-colored, Italian leather tote and stood as the train rocked to a stop. Rolling her tight shoulders, she slipped the tote strap over her head cross-body and checked herself in a full-length mirror at the end of the car. Always considered beautiful, Eve had been overweight in middle and high schools, and she was always on guard for any extra weight. She told people it was because, as a fashion designer, it was important to stay thin, but she knew it was more than that. Childhood taunts still haunted her. The ghost was always in the shadows. Approving what she saw, Eve disembarked with a wave and "*bon soirée*" to the car attendant.

Her mouth curved into a smile as she remembered she'd arranged to have her luggage delivered to the hotel. The additional cost had made her pause when she first considered it, but the freedom to move around the city without dragging a giant suitcase over cobblestones and uneven sidewalks was definitely worth it. And Eve-M

Fashions was finally clearing enough to allow her a few business-related perks.

Normally she might have preferred a taxi, but the queue for taxis was long and it was June in Paris. The warm evening encouraged her to walk to the hotel. She rummaged in her purse for the directions and headed to an ATM to retrieve euros. A measure of her energy returned at the smell of fresh flowers from a neighboring kiosk. The wide sidewalks of Paris, the smells of the cafés, the people moving, all cheered her. She smiled as she looked forward to her little adventure. Eve bought a small bouquet of flowers, inhaled the fragrance, then handed it to a young girl who had been mesmerized by the flowers at the kiosk.

"For you, mademoiselle."

The little girl's mouth and eyes opened wide. "*Oh! Merci, madame! Merci beaucoup!*"

Eve smiled, happy she could make the girl's day with such a small gift. Then, she rechecked her directions and headed out of the station. The directions indicated the hotel was only about ten minutes' walk, and after the ride on the train, she needed a bit of exercise.

She was walking down a quiet, shadowed side street when she heard men talking behind her. Their voices were low and gaining on her quickly. A glance over her shoulder confirmed they were staring at her and there were no other people on the street. She checked the doorways ahead of her, searching for a café or shop to slip into until they passed, but this seemed to be a residential block.

Rough laughter caused fear to jangle her core. She quickened her pace and thought, *I should have taken a taxi.*

Quickening steps were landing ever closer to her, and panic seized her. Her heart pounded. Her hands trembled. *Where can I run?* Despite the alarm that was fast consuming her, she started to turn and confront the men when a large heavy hand landed on her shoulder.

"*Mademoiselle*," the rough voice almost growled, as she was turned toward the men. Both were unshaven, unkempt, and smelled of alcohol. The hand on her was big, rough, and dirty.

"Leave me alone," Eve managed to get out, but she wasn't even convincing to herself.

"*Mademoiselle parle anglais*," the bigger of the two said. He had a two-inch red scar down the right side of his face. "In that case, madame, we insist" – the word "insist" was slurred by his drunken state – "on being, what, Maurice? Oh yes, good ambassadors and welcome you to Paris." The man's hand was still on her shoulder, the pressure not relenting.

With no other people around and the sun quickly disappearing, the cheerful Paris of a few minutes ago was now very scary.

"Oh, there you are," came a voice from behind the two men. "I missed you at the station. I hoped I could catch up. *Pardon, monsieurs, la dame était perdue – ma copine. S'il vous plaît.*" With that, an athletic man with light brown hair put his arm around her shoulder and slid her out of the grasp of her molesters. "*Merci*," he said over his shoulder, as he whisked her away, around a corner and into a café a few steps away.

"Really, dear, you shouldn't worry me so – going off like that without your phone or the directions." He was saying this loudly enough to be heard by the two now bewildered looking derelicts, who looked at them, then each other, then turned, with heads down and walked a distance away, as if to discuss their options.

"Who, what, uh," was about all Eve was able to get out while she gasped to catch her breath.

"Oh, hi! I should probably introduce myself," he said. "I'm Michael – Michael Thomas. And you, lovely lady?"

"Uh Eve, Eve Belot."

"Well, Uh Eve, I didn't mean to pull you away in that overly familiar fashion, but you looked like you needed a rescue – I mean your gentleman friends didn't seem to be dressed for the occasion, whatever the occasion is – or was going to be."

"No, it's not uh Eve, just Eve. And, thank you. I don't think those, as you put it, gentlemen had anything gentle on their minds. How did . . ."

"Well, just Eve, "I'd hoped to find you at the station, but I was delayed. John and Meg gave me your train number. Glad I was able to find you when I did."

"Not 'just Eve,' it's just – Eve."

"That's what I said, just Eve. Anyway, those two are going to hang around to be sure I didn't just rescue you and you are going to be out and 'available prey' again, so I would suggest that we have a glass of wine, maybe a nosh or two – strictly my treat, of course, and all in the name of safety."

"Only if you get my name right," she said, smiling for the first time.

"Perfect. I knew if I made myself irritating enough, you'd start to forget about those two and smile."

Eve laughed. She noticed his hair, medium length, light brown. His eyes were blue – a penetrating blue – blue you could get lost in. He was tan, and a loose-fitting shirt couldn't hide an athletic physique. She guessed he was just under six feet tall.

The waiter appeared. "*Monsieur*," Michael said, "would you please bring a menu, *s'il vous plaît* ."

Ten minutes later, they were sipping a glass of wine and nibbling on a cheese plate.

"Well, I certainly didn't think this is how the day would end," said Eve. "And I really didn't think it would end this way about fifteen minutes ago. So, you're the friend in Paris who suggested the hotel?"

"Yes," he said. "My place isn't too far from here and I'd hoped to meet your train. At least I knew the hotel and decided to walk over. They said you'd want a place where you could research the latest fashions."

"Yes. I'm a fashion designer, for our small-ish business back in the U.S. Every year, I come to places in Europe to get an idea of what is in and what is not."

"And you use those ideas back home?"

"I don't pirate, but I get an idea of where the designs are going, and use that." *And,* she thought, *we could use some new ideas or a new line.*

She thought about the business, and her best friend, Meg. Now Meg, John, and their two children lived in suburbia, and – sadly, she thought – they didn't see each other as often. A closeness that she missed, even as she was happy for her friend. Whenever she thought of it, there was a growing hollowness within her.

"And you, what is it that brings you here and what do you do – other than save the occasional – I'm assuming occasional," Eve laughed, "damsel in distress?"

"I work for a publisher who pays me to go to various places throughout Europe, write – mostly travel pieces, but other things, too. My work is in their magazines. It helps build their other businesses, as well. Since you know John, you know the job. When John got married, he gave up his gig here. I became the semi-anonymous writer Digby - the writer whose face is never seen."

Eve started to laugh, then cough. "Oh, my! YOU'RE the new Digby!"

"At your service, ma'am."

Two

Their encounter had gone from wine and noshes to a small dinner, with a small seasonal salad and a poached white fish. He'd gone to the counter for bread, and returning, took his time to take in her perfect figure.

Not trying to be obvious, he noticed the perfect curve of her jaw, her cute nose, her gorgeous blond hair, and her pale and perfect complexion. She was leaning against the table and he drank in the way her back curved gently down to her hips and derriere. From there, perfect legs curved back under the wrought iron chair. He hoped she hadn't noticed when he'd walked into a chair on the way back to the table – a result of paying more attention to her than to the path back.

"So, Mr. Thomas, tell me more about your Digby gig," she said when he'd returned from the counter. Eve had relaxed when she found she'd been rescued by a friend – at least someone trusted by a friend.

"Not much to tell. If you know John Kelly, then you must know something about it."

She sat back, sipping the white wine that he'd had ordered with the fish. A cool breeze and a delightful meal with this delicious wine made her feel at ease. The handsome former stranger who had saved her gave her a warm happy feeling.

"I travel around and, like John did, I live with the so-called common people who make up the areas I'm visiting. I stay for a while and learn from them about where they live – the things that are of interest, the history. Most of the things I write are travel pieces, but there are other more in-depth assignments, as well. I've done a few exposés."

"And, what if there isn't anything of interest?"

"Every place has a story," said Michael. "There is always something that makes it unique." He paused and got a faraway look in his eyes. "Sometimes it is a sad story, sometimes a happy one."

Eve decided to relent – a bit. "And when you're not traveling, where is home?"

"I've got a small – and I do mean small – place here in Paris. As a comedian once put it, the place is so small the mice have to go out into the hall to change their minds."

She laughed. "It can't be that bad."

"About 600 square feet. I don't need much. A lot of my time is spent traveling, so there isn't a need for a large place, and I don't have to spend the money for one."

"And, is this Digby job one that rotates through various writers?"

"Well, I know there was at least one before John. He's – John – a good guy. We keep in touch – not often, but regularly enough. I do miss the guy." Michael paused, "The job is like the movie <u>Princess Bride</u> with the legendary dread pirate. One guy holds the job until he gets too old or too rich – only here, it's usually just too old, or something happens –

like John and Meg. Then, the protégé takes his place and voila, the ever-youthful pirate, er, writer. That's the reason we've all used the same by-line. Different writers can rotate through the role seamlessly. And, from time to time, there are actually more than one Digby."

Eve thought back to when she met John, and how he and her best friend, Meg, had gotten together, then married. "Yes, a great guy. I don't see Meg - outside of work – or John, as often as I would like." She sipped her wine. "He had an interesting story, you know, the way he fell into the Digby character, essentially an outcast after killing a man who attacked his future wife."

"Yes, he told me. I'm glad it worked out for him – and Meg – in the end."

"So, do all Digby's have an interesting story, you know, how they got here?"

"Well, the guy before John had a story. I guess we all have a story."

"As interesting as John's?"

"We all have a story. Most probably aren't as – how did you say, interesting, as John's, but I doubt that any of us lucky enough to fill the role is here because he was born with a silver spoon in his mouth or doesn't have anything better to do with his time."

"So, will you tell me your story?"

"Mine isn't a particularly happy story. It would

probably be better if that were saved for another time." She noticed that as he said this, he looked away, then remained silent. She regretted pushing him for something he wasn't ready to share.

Finally, he turned. "So, tell me more about your trip to Paris, where you'll go and what you'll do. If it works out, I'd love to have the pleasure of your company again."

"Why, thank you. I'm afraid it isn't very glamorous. I'll spend some time looking in the shop windows – you know to see what they are selling, then, I'll spend time watching what the women are really wearing. Sometimes there is a great difference between what is in a shop and on a body."

"Perfect. If you don't mind, I'll walk you to your hotel tonight and collect you there in the morning – about 9, or is 10 better? We can do the window shopping and after have lunch in an outdoor café while we watch the fashion parade."

"I wouldn't want to have you waste your day on me," she said, actually pleased that he would join her.

"It would be my pleasure. I'm off assignment for a bit, and this will be a treat for me."

As they left the restaurant. Eve tried to tell Michael that she could probably make it to her hotel without an escort, but she tripped on a piece of broken sidewalk, and he caught her as she started to fall. She gripped his arm, which she found was nicely shaped and as hard as granite.

"Perhaps, Madame, I can still be of some assistance," he said gallantly.

"Yes, well, perhaps," she said and smiled, grateful that he was there to catch her.

They walked to her hotel, he said "*Bon soirée*" and promised to be there in the morning.

Eve walked to the reception desk, a smile on her face. Her attraction to this man who had saved her – twice – since she had arrived was something to consider. She had a friend in Paris, and it made the city all that more comfortable.

She checked into her room and found her luggage had been delivered. It took a few minutes to unpack. She'd learned to pack light and found clothes you could actually wad and throw into the corner for a couple of days, after which, they'd still look good.

Mandatory work done for the night, she showered and dressed in her night clothes. It was late enough to go to bed, but she didn't feel like sleeping. She opened the window and looked at the street scene below. Sounds of people in the night, loud enough to be heard but quiet enough not to be a disturbance, filled the room. After her evening with Michael, she was thinking of Meg and John.

The mention of John had sent a tingle through her body. *Maybe that's why I'm still awake.* John had been like a tidal wave. She'd never felt like that about anyone before, and she'd started to want what her friend had. With success and comfort in life, she'd discovered she wanted a committed relationship, and eventually, children.

Eve thought about Michael. Maybe it was Paris and the sense of adventure. He was a nice enough guy. He HAD saved her from – from something that she was sure wouldn't have ended well. That much she knew. But for now, he was only an interesting guy.

She crawled into bed and turned off the light.

Three

The phone rang three times before it was picked up.

"Hi, Meg? It's Eve."

"Eve! I just got home. How's Paris? How was London?"

"London was great. I will have to admit that I think I wore myself out. I caught a couple of shows that I probably shouldn't have and stayed up too late."

"All work and no play."

"That's what I thought, but maybe I'm getting old . . ."

"More likely you have a picture growing old in the attic. You know you're as beautiful now as ever."

"Anyway," continued Eve, "I got a few really good ideas – at least I think they are really good – while I was in London. Let's hope I can do the same here."

"You always have great ideas and fashion sense. I wish I had your talent."

"Well, Meg, you're the one with the business sense. Without you, I'd be sitting around looking at fashions and eating Ramen noodles. By the way, my visit to Paris started off with a bit of excitement."

"Good excitement or bad excitement?"

"A little of both. I decided to walk from Gare de Nord to the hotel. It was a beautiful night in Paris."

"Don't rub it in."

"Well, the sun was setting faster than I thought, and the area I was in was a bit deserted. Two men – drunk, big, and dirty – "

"Oh, no!"

"Oh yes, oh no. Anyway, they apparently wanted me to go with them for a drink – likely out of a dirty wine bottle – and some 'fun' afterward."

"You must have been terrified!"

"I passed terrified when the guy put his hand on my shoulder. Panicked was more like it."

"So, what did you do?"

"I didn't do much of anything. All of a sudden, a nice-looking guy butts in between these two, puts his arm around me, tells the two Neanderthals that he's been looking for me all over, and guides me into a café about half a block away."

"Why . .? How . .?"

"I don't know. I thought he just happened to be there and saw what was going on. He took a chance with those two, although I get the idea he could hold his own if he had to."

"So . . ."

"He told me that to keep up the ruse, we should have a bottle of wine and something to eat."

"Uh huh."

"It wasn't like that. I felt totally safe with this guy. He was a perfect gentleman. Turns out, he writes for a magazine, and if I give you a guess, you can probably tell me what his byline is. As a hint, he's frequently photographed in front of landmarks, but you only see the back of his head."

"Oh my God, Eve! I don't believe it!" Meg was laughing. "In all of Europe. But I don't think I quite understand."

"Well, when John gave up the Digby gig to – you know, marry you and settle down – they had someone else in mind – or found someone else. He says he knows John. His name is Michael. Michael Thomas."

"Hold on." Meg pulled her head away from the phone. "John!"

Through the phone, Eve overheard her friend's conversation.

John Kelly bent around the doorway. "Yes?"

"Eve says she ran into someone you know – in Paris. Michael Thomas?"

"Oh, yes, Michael. I know Michael. He was going to meet Eve's train. Problem?"

"Long story. I'll tell you later. So, who is this Michael?"

"They always have a Digby," said John. "In fact, they kind of have one, and one in training, sort of. When I wanted to marry you, and thank you for marrying me, I knew keeping the job as Digby wouldn't be possible. Michael was doing some stories, and he took over."

"So, what is his story? And, by the way, you're welcome – for the marrying thing."

"What do you mean?"

"You told me once that you weren't writing stories as Digby because you'd won the lottery and didn't know what to do with your time." Meg returned to the phone for a moment, "Eve, dear, just a few seconds, I'm trying to find out something about Michael. John is being somewhat obstructionist."

"He said he had a story," said Eve, "but he said it was not a particularly happy story and last night wasn't the time to tell it."

"Okay," said Meg, turning again to John, "so what is his story?"

"Everyone who works as Digby has a story. Most are trying to put something behind them, or like me, trying to survive because they can't be where they would like to be otherwise."

"So?"

"If you or Eve want to know Michael's story, you'll have to get it from him. If, and when he decides he wants to share it, he will. But I wouldn't push him. He'll only share it if he feels safe enough and the person he shares it with is someone he trusts – completely."

Meg returned her attention to the phone. "Eve, I'll try to worm this out of John. If I get anything, I'll let you know. In the meantime, have some fun. Are you planning to see Michael again?"

"Yes, actually, he is supposed to pick me up shortly. Was supposed to be at ten, we've pushed it to later. We'll do some window shopping. Then, as he said, have a leisurely lunch at an outdoor café and watch the fashions walk by."

"I'd say don't overwork yourself, but I need to check the mirror to see if I'm turning green."

"You are doing perfectly well where you are and with the man you have there."

"Well, I meant Paris, outdoor café, all that, but you are right, I'm doing well here. Call me later, Eve, and let me know how it is going. I love you, dear."

"Love you, too."

Four

Eve and Michael sat under the red awning outside of Fouquet's café, on the Champs-Elysees. It was just after noon, and they were enjoying a light lunch, with the ever-present bottle of wine. Eve had decided to wear a strapless high low print dress – white with a blue paisley print. While she knew they were going to be walking, she decided on a rhinestone flat. She had a silver bangle set on her right wrist. Michael wore a solid dark blue short-sleeved button-up silk shirt and black slacks. Gray woven loafers completed his look.

Not bad, thought Eve, when he picked her up at her hotel. *Classic, and not trying too hard. And, much better than t-shirt, shorts, and running shoes.*

"You look lovely," he'd said. "We're going to be walking, will your shoes be okay? Not that I would want to question a woman's choice of wardrobe."

"You're probably right, but I think I'll be okay. Besides, you should know how important it is to have the right look. This outfit just wouldn't do with a pair of clunky shoes."

He'd been right, of course. Her feet were sore. At least he had the good sense not to notice or mention it, although they did need to stop fairly frequently – he said for his convenience.

As they'd walked along, Eve had taken notes, and a few

pictures. Some things she'd just noted in her mind. Now, they were sipping a rosé wine from Provence. She had ordered a small summer salad and a petite quiche Lorraine. He had ordered a salade niçoise with tuna. The weather was warm, but not hot. A gentle breeze wafted the fragrance of nearby flowers to the table.

"So," started Michael, "tell me about Eve."

"Eve Belot," she answered. "My father was French. My mother Scandinavian. I grew up in the San Francisco area. Life was pretty good until my father, who worked as the manager of a bank, ran off with one of his assistants. When I graduated high school, I went off to a small college to study fashion design. It was there that I met my business partner and started a small fashion business. I do the designing, and she takes care of the business end. A few years ago, an article came out in a magazine called Fashion Week, and business took off. That's also how John was able to find Meg after all those years – but you probably know that part already."

Michael sipped his wine and turned to look across the street. Eve didn't see anything that needed his rapt attention, and she figured he must be thinking of something. "Penny for your thoughts?"

Michael's attention returned. "Oh, I'm sorry. I'm not much of a luncheon partner. Something you said triggered a thought."

"You'll have to tell me what it was. First, however, tell me about Michael Thomas."

"Not much to tell. My mother is English. Beatrice Thomas. A lovely woman."

Eve tried to look casual and took a sip of wine after asking, "And your father?"

"Not sure."

"You don't know his name?" she asked and took another sip of wine.

"Oh, I know his name alright. Handsome Stranger."

Eve coughed. Only grabbing her napkin and covering her mouth kept her from spitting wine all over the table. She started to laugh and said, "The least you could have done is wait until I swallowed."

"True, but, and pardon my honesty, you're even adorable when you have wine coming out your nose. I am sorry, but sometimes I have this overpowering need to . . ."

"Make someone look like an idiot? Thank God it wasn't champagne. You know, I'm going to have to find some way to get you back for this."

"That's half the fun. Waiting for the other shoe to drop. Besides, that way, I figure you'll have to see me again. I just have to watch out for land mines."

By now, they were both laughing. And, not wanting to have the afternoon end too quickly, Michael ordered a cheese plate.

"Okay, you got me with that one. So, after Handsome

Stranger?"

He thought for a moment. "When my mom was pregnant with me, she moved to the States. I was born a resident. She worked at the National Library of Medicine – you know at the National Institutes of Health. I went to high school in Rockville, just up the road. I went to community college and transferred to the University of Maryland, where I got a degree in engineering. I opened a business." He remained silent. "Mom moved back to the UK."

Eve took a small bite of cheese and sipped her wine. After a minute, she said, "Then, something happened."

He looked at her, then looked away. "Yes. Then something happened."

As if the universe knew the 'something' was not good, the sky clouded over and the wind picked up.

Michael looked around then said, "It looks like the weather may be changing. We should probably get you back to your hotel."

Eve decided not to pry, but said, "It has been so lovely – this morning and lunch. I really don't want it to end just yet. Is there somewhere we could go – inside?"

He seemed subdued. "Sure. I know just the place."

They started back toward Eve's hotel. After a while, Michael directed Eve to a small café just as rain began to fall, slowly at first, then forcefully. They went inside. Michael was greeted by the owner.

"*Monsieur Thomas. Bienvienue!* Who is your lovely friend?"

"*Claude, je tu presente Eve Belot.* Eve is from the United States – here to see what fashions we have."

"Well, welcome Madame! Any friend of Michael's is more than welcome here. Lucien!"

A waiter appeared.

"*Ah, Lucien! Une bouteille de vin blanc, s'il vous plait.*"

Lucien went off. Eve turned to Michael, "Your special place?"

"Yes, I come here often – when I'm home. They're like family."

Lucien returned with a bottle of Chablis. Then, he put a basket of bread on the table.

Michael poured the wine and chatted with Claude for a moment. He offered Claude some wine, which Claude declined. Claude said something that Eve couldn't quite hear then departed.

"Anything of interest?"

"No. Not really. But the French are much more social than Americans. That's one of the reasons there is some animosity when Americans come here."

"What do you mean?"

"Your typical American tourist seems to think that the world either does or should run on American values. They will come into a shop in a huff, paw through the merchandise for the best deal, and if they don't find what they want, they leave in a huff." Michael sipped his wine. "On the other hand, the French are much more social. When you enter a shop, you will hear *'Bon jour.'* It is polite to respond with *'Bon jour,'* as well. Then, there is an expected bit of social interaction – even if the place is mobbed. Americans don't do things that way. They want it Wham, Bam, Thank you Ma'am. That irritates the bejesus out of the people here. To tell you the truth, I'm not sure how well I'd do back home anymore."

"I'm sure you would do fine. But back to Paris, you've wined and dined me – and it wasn't cheap. You should let me share the cost."

"Never. Do I offer money when I come to your place?"

"You've never been to my place, but as I was saying, this isn't cheap. I can write this off, you know, not pay taxes on business expenses. And, Eve-M is doing well enough to do that. Let me help."

"Nope. First, I do okay. I'm paid reasonably well. When I'm 'on a job,' not only do I get my usual pay, I'm also on expenses, so I kind of live for free – plus pay. And, I'm on the job most of the time. Second, being with you today had nothing to do with tax write-offs or business expenses. I wanted to be with you."

Eve smiled and said, "Thank you. This is wonderful.

You've been so nice."

"I feel a 'but' coming on."

"No. No buts, no howevers, no caveats." Eve's head was not affected by the little bit of wine they'd had, but she was thrilled this man was with her and wanted to be with her. There was a tingling in her arms and legs that had nothing to do with the wine.

"Besides," he added, "who is going to protect you from the drunken Parisian marauders?"

Eve rolled her eyes and said, "Well, you have to let me take you to dinner to make up for this."

"Here's an idea, instead. How about I actually make dinner for you – say, tomorrow evening?"

"You can cook?"

"I'm not great, but we should both live through the experience, and it might be fun."

They left their table, leaving the unfinished wine. "Claude, could you please call a taxi for the lady? And, again, I am sorry, but I was unable to finish the wine. Would you ask the staff if they would, *s'il vous plait*?"

"*Oui, monsieur*," he said with a smile. "They are always happy to do this little task for you."

"Here. This is my cell number," he said to her, giving her a card with the number written on the back. When Eve turned it over, on the front of the business card was the name

Brian Spencer.

"So, who is Brian Spencer, and why are you giving me his card?"

"You should know from John that when a story is done, it is done. Many times, people will want to get in touch – or just complain. If they call the number, they will get the voice mail of Brian Spencer. If it is important, I'll call back. Mostly, it isn't important. And, I don't want everyone to have my cell phone number."

"Just special someones?" she couldn't resist. She wanted to hear it.

"Just a very special someone," he said, and a warm fuzzy feeling filled her. "And," he added, "please don't write it on any ladies' room walls – you know, to get back for the wine out the nose."

"Oooo. I almost forgot about that."

When the taxi arrived, Michael told the driver to take Eve to the Hotel Opera Cadet, 24 rue Cadet, then he paid the driver. More likely, he greatly overpaid the driver, who was profuse in his thanks.

Five

As soon as Eve got back to the hotel, she called Meg at the office. The time difference was six hours.

"Eve, how are things going? Seeing anything interesting in Paris?"

"Um, yes. Some very interesting things. Fashions, too."

Meg paused, then said, "O-k-a-y. I take it you've seen Mr. Michael Thomas again. So how did it go?"

"It went really, really well, but . . ."

"Really, really well, but what?"

"He started to talk about his mom and not knowing his father."

"He didn't know his father?"

"No. And when I asked him if he knew his name, he said he did. He waited until I had wine in my mouth and told me his father's name was 'handsome stranger.' I ended up spitting wine and blowing it out my nose."

"Not a good look on anyone, but hilarious, anyway."

"A lot you know. He said I looked adorable, even with wine coming out my nose. I told him I'd get him back for that."

"It sounds like you two were having a great time."

"Yes, we were. Then, he told me about going to school and opening a business. Well, I know everyone who has a Digby job has something in his past, so I said, 'Then, something happened.' And his whole mood changed. God, I hope I didn't screw it up. It's not like I'm making wedding plans, but he's a great guy, and I didn't want to hurt him. Meg? Meg, are you there?"

"I'm here. Yes, I don't know. You should probably tread very lightly on any issue he might have had. I mean if he is that sensitive about it, he'd have to feel closer, you know, to trust you more. So, he doesn't get hurt."

"You know what it is, don't you?"

"What? No. God! John made me promise – he really made me promise. He said if you had any idea what it was, you'd give yourself away. And he'd lose a really great friend, and if you two ever had a chance, it would go away, too. I can't. I really want to, but I can't. If anything happened, I'd feel worse about that than I feel about not telling you – if it is even possible to feel worse."

"Can't you give me any hints?"

"Eve, why are you doing this to me?"

"Because I don't want to hurt this guy. I don't know if anything will happen between us, but he's great to be with, and I don't want to say or do anything that would hurt him."

"I can't TELL you anything."

"But, if I guess, and you don't answer, then I'm getting

closer, right?"

"Eve! Please!"

"Okay. Here we go. He doesn't know who his father is. So, is it something to do with that?"

"Eve, I can't."

"So, that's not it. His mom went back to the UK, so they are estranged, or something."

"I'm not doing this."

"Somebody embezzled and ruined his business – and the law is chasing him."

"Eve, I said . . ."

"Oh, crap! There's only one thing left. Some woman put a knife through his heart. The way he reacted, the knife is still in there. That's it, isn't it? Meg? Meg, are you there? Of course not. Bingo, sort of. Why are women always screwing up my life?"

"Wait a minute. What other women have screwed up your life?"

She hoped Meg didn't hear her gulp. It wasn't Meg's fault that Meg and John were together – well, sort of it was. But they did belong together. It was just that Eve felt she could have been deliriously happy with John, as well.

"What other women have screwed up your life?" the question was asked a bit more forcefully.

"It's just an expression. Besides, we're still on me. So, what did this – we'll call her a woman for now, although I have a different word in mind – woman do to hurt him so badly that he left for another continent and cringes at the thought of the wound? There are only so many ways a woman can screw a guy up this badly. Jealousy? Betrayal? Really BIG betrayal? Meg?"

"Eve! Stop it! I already did more than I should have. I'm trapped here. You're my best friend ever. But I also promised John, and according to him, telling you will only make things worse. Please trust me. And, if you ask any more questions, I'll just hang up."

"Fine. Then, I'll just have to . . ." Eve was trying to say as Meg started blocking her words with "Blah, blah, blah, blah," over and over, again.

"Real mature, Meg. Okay, I get it."

"Look, I really want you to have a good time over there. Just take it easy."

"Easy for you to say. You've got John."

"I almost didn't. Are you saying you want Michael?"

"I don't know. Maybe. He's a gentleman. He's protective without being jealous. He's smart. And, there's just something about him."

"Why don't you just charm him?" Eve's ability to charm men was legendary. When she wanted to be, she was totally irresistible.

"Because, for some reason, charming him would be like tricking him, and I don't want to trick him. I think I actually care about him. Besides, I'm not sure he's susceptible. Maybe I'm losing my touch."

"I'm not sure any man is immune to Eve Belot's charm," said Meg. "When will you see him again?"

"He's cooking dinner for me – at his place. Tomorrow night."

"You'd better get some sleep, Eve."

"Yeah. Right. Sleep. While I try to figure out how this witch ruined him for any other woman."

"If anybody can do it, baby, my money is on you. Now go to bed – sleep. I love you."

"I love you too – even if you are incredibly close-mouthed."

Six

The day had been beautiful in Paris. Eve had spent most of it looking in shop windows or wandering the streets – with map in hand – to try to see what people were wearing rather than what was in the fashion store windows. While there were many beautiful fashions in the Paris windows, many weren't what the ladies were wearing. Eve-M specialized in trendy fashions for working women. Style, comfort, ease of care, and durability were all important, and Eve was the one person on whose shoulders rested the success or failure of the fashion business.

It was about 4:30 when she arrived at Michael's apartment house. The building was old, older than probably anything in the U.S. It had a gray stone façade. Eve found the apartment number and pressed the buzzer. She was met with, "Hello, welcome. Please take the lift to the sixth floor." She entered the building and found the lift, looking like something out of a 1930s movie. It had an open cage and an accordion door. She opened the door, stepped in, pulled the door closed, and pushed the button – hoping against hope that it would work. The elevator started immediately and ran smoothly to the sixth floor.

Michael was waiting for her when the elevator stopped. "Welcome to my little home. I hope it is comfortable for you." He opened the door. He was wearing faded jeans and a cashmere sweater. She was glad she had chosen to go casual, as well, with a pair of dark blue slacks and a pink sleeveless sweater.

The apartment was masculine, without being overpowering. *No woman ever lived here*, she thought, *although that's what he was running from. I don't think he's been serious since – although how I would know that, I don't know.*

She could see the apartment was indeed small – maybe not even 600 square feet. The bedroom door was slightly ajar, showing a room with a queen-size bed, probably a closet and dresser as well – not much else. Another door, again, slightly ajar identified the bathroom. It looked small. The kitchen was larger than she suspected it would be, but then, again, this was Paris. What she could see of the cooking implements were high end. The rest of the apartment was taken up with a living space and small dining space – just enough room for two. The floors were hardwood. A Persian rug covered most of the floor. A sofa faced the window that covered the one side of the apartment. Side chairs and a small coffee table against the window completed the conversation group with the sofa. In the corner, a spiral staircase that led to – where?

Michael was saying something, although she'd missed it during her musing. "I'm sorry, I was looking at the apartment and totally missed what you were saying."

"No problem, beautiful women frequently ignore me," he said with a smile. "I was just saying that the building was completed in the 1800s, but it has been completely updated – well, at least the conveniences that count, in the last ten years. You know, elevator, plumbing – you don't have to go out back, for example."

Eve laughed. "Well, I'm glad for that. You'd have to plan your trips if the elevator was busy." She handed him a small bouquet of flowers and a bottle of wine. "For you, *Monsieur*."

"*Merci beaucoup, Madame*."

"So, may I ask what you have planned for dinner?"

"Certainly. I thought we would start with a small libation and fruit. Then, a salad – summer greens. And, I thought I would try out a recipe for chicken with Calvados sauce."

"Calvados?"

"Yes. It's an apple brandy, but don't worry, the alcohol cooks off in the process."

She tilted her head just a bit and put a smile on her lips. *Well, just for the heck of it, let's see if the old charm works – I mean if I have to use it at some point, I might as well know. Not too much, just a test.* "Kind of a shame, letting all that alcohol go, isn't it?" For emphasis, she let her hand brush against his forearm.

"Not really. It's the flavor we are after. I have wine for alcohol."

Rats! She thought. *I got a reaction, but it wasn't nearly what I usually get.* She wasn't too upset, she'd told the truth when she said she didn't want – to put it crudely – to charm the pants off the guy.

"Would you like to help? Or at least keep me company

while I cook? We can chat."

"I'd love to." And she realized she meant it. "But I'll watch. I've been known to burn water, and I don't want to mess up the meal."

"But first, a bit of champagne." He deftly opened a bottle of Moet & Chandon and poured two glasses. He also had a plate of fresh berries, pear, and apple. Something to nosh while they drank and he cooked.

He prepared a fresh summer salad using romaine lettuce, onion, cucumber, apple, and thinly sliced radishes. He took long enough, purposely, so that they were able to chat. He placed the salads on the small dining table.

Then, he started wild rice cooking slowly and began his main dish, chicken with calvados.

At the small table, he served Eve the salad and a plate with the rice and chicken. He chose a sauvignon blanc for the wine.

"This is really lovely," she said. "You cook better than most of the restaurants back home." She started to say he would make some woman a wonderful husband someday, but she realized that could be a minefield, and she didn't want to spoil this evening.

"Thank you. I don't have much of a chance to cook for anyone else. When I'm on the job, I'm usually living where I don't do the cooking – unless it is over a campfire – and when I'm here, I don't have many guests."

"That's really a shame," she said. "You're a great cook, and your talents shouldn't be hidden." As she said it, she realized that she was secretly happy that he wasn't cooking for anyone else. She felt a little bad about that, but then realized she was just happy there wasn't anyone he was seeing.

They were just finishing dinner when Michael's cell phone rang. He walked over, picked it up, and looked at the screen. "I'm sorry. I need to take this."

"Do you need me to leave?" Eve asked, knowing she didn't want to leave.

"No. No. Please. I just hate to take calls on the rare occasions that I entertain. Please. This shouldn't take long. Enjoy the wine."

He stepped to the other side of the room, punched the phone, put it to his ear and said, "Thomas." Eve was surprised at how business-like his response was. All she could hear was his side of the conversation. But she was amazed that he considered her in this interruption. Back home, a call would have been taken without even acknowledging the 'live' guest in the room.

"No."

"A young woman I met – here. Turns out she is a friend of John Kelly, as well."

"Yes."

"Okay. What's the gig?" There was a long pause.

"At least this one sounds like it will be more fun." Pause.

"That might be tough. I'll be easy to spot."

Michael turned and looked at Eve. "What if . . . What if I could arrange something?"

"Maybe. I'll have to check. I think I'll be able to let you know tomorrow."

"Yes, either way."

"You too. Bye."

He punched the phone, then held the button that turned it off.

"Aren't you afraid you will miss a call?" asked Eve.

"I won't get any more tonight."

"Another job?"

"Yes."

"When?"

"Three days."

Her heart sank. While she wasn't quite ready to commit, she was having more fun than she'd had in a long time, and she didn't want it to end. She also wanted more time to be with Michael – to see if they could click. And three days wasn't going to be enough time to find out what his issue was.

Seven

Eve was finishing her glass of wine. Michael came over and said, "Was dinner okay?"

"Dinner was magnificent, Michael. You must know that. I haven't had a meal that delicious in I don't know how long. Why did you ask?"

"I just wanted to know if you enjoyed it."

"The company more than the meal."

He smiled. "Have you had too much to drink?"

"Not by a long shot. If you're trying to ply me with liquor . . ." Eve batted her eyes, flipped her hair, and gave a coquettish smile. The effect was so overdone, as she had hoped, it made Michael laugh out loud.

"Well, then, I have something I think you would like to see." He led her to the small spiral staircase and up the stairs. At the top, he opened a door, and they left the interior of his apartment to stand on a small roof garden where they could see much of the city.

"Oh, my," she said. "This is absolutely beautiful. It's, it's – I don't know. Beyond words."

"Yes, it is nice. And I do love the view."

Michael opened a small panel and inside was the unfinished bottle of champagne – which he'd brought up using a hidden dumb waiter. "You must be careful on the way down the steps. When it is time, I will go first. If you fall, you will have something soft to land on."

Joy rushed through her and she impulsively kissed his cheek. Michael blushed. Then, he poured the champagne and pulled out two chairs.

The sun was setting and the lights of the city were coming on. She could see the Eiffel Tower in the distance. "This is so beautiful, I could stay here forever."

Michael was looking at her. His gaze hadn't left her in at least two minutes. Finally, he said, "Yes, very beautiful. Very beautiful, indeed. I am a lucky man."

She blushed and looked away. Her heart did a flip, and there was a tingle inside her. She had to say something. "So, you have another job?" She knew it was lame.

"Yes."

"In three days?" She wasn't doing any better. But Michael was seemingly half there, half lost in thought.

"Yes, three days."

"I want you to know that three days doesn't seem very long, and I'll miss you – when those three days are up." *That was better – not so lame.*

"Yes, this time together has been wonderful for me."

She put her hand on his forearm and said, "Yes. Wonderful for me, as well."

"Well then, before we drink any more, perhaps I should ask you something – well, somethings."

Her heart was pounding in her chest. *"What could he want to ask? What did he want to do?"* Her mind was racing.

"Um, sure. What did you have – uh – want to ask?" *Oh, god, I'm back to lame.*

"I've got this job coming up in three days. Don't say anything until I finish, okay?"

"Oh, of course." *"No wonder I'm still single. Light conversation just doesn't seem to be my thing – tonight anyway, when it REALLY counts."*

"I'm supposed to get a story on a guy. He's not supposed to know I'm getting the story."

"You're going undercover?"

"Sort of, well, yes, but it isn't dangerous undercover. I'll just assume another name and occupation."

"Okay."

"The guy is a congressman."

"Yikes!"

"They all put their pants on the same way." Michael laughed. "Or in this case, take them off. Anyway, this congressman is over here, well not that far from here, on a vacation. He's calling it a working vacation back home, but nobody there seems to know where he is or what he's doing."

"Go on." Eve was interested.

"As it turns out, he is on vacation with a young woman, at least twenty years his junior, while his wife and three children are home in the states. Oh, yes, as you can imagine, he's a guy who runs on a family values platform – and voted against a lot of things that are now considered mainstream."

"And your job is to get the proof?"

"My job is to write a story telling about his European vacation."

"I don't know why you didn't want me to say anything until you finished. Go after him. He sounds like a sleaze."

"Yeah, he actually got another young woman pregnant and paid her to get an abortion. The abortion and another ten thousand in hush money."

"So, go after him."

"Well, the thing is, the two of them will be on a river cruise. Small floating love nest."

Eve just looked.

"So, here's the deal. If you can spare about ten days, and are willing to come along, I'd like to have you on the cruise with me. Wait. We will have to pretend to be married or cohabitating and share a stateroom. We can make sure the sleeping arrangements are acceptable to you – I can sleep on the floor. We'll both wear something appropriate to sleep in.

It shouldn't be too hard. And, I'll get to spend a little more time with you. You by the way, for putting up with me, will get a free river cruise."

Eve sat stunned. All she could do is stare.

"They wanted to get somebody to act as my wife, and I thought you might enjoy first, the river cruise, and second, seeing one of the things Digby does. Hello?"

"What? Wait. Well, yes. YES, I'd love to. But I don't think I could act like, you know, someone else."

"That's the beauty of it. You really don't have to. You can be Eve Belot, principal designer for Eve-M fashions. You've already got all that backstory."

"What about you? If you say you're, even if you say you're Brian Spencer, they're going to duck and cover as soon as they hear you're with a news agency."

"But I won't be Brian Spencer – or Michael Thomas. I'll be George Franklin, an insurance broker."

"What if they start asking you questions? Do you know enough about insurance to fool them?"

Michael started to laugh. "Don't be silly. If somebody says they are in insurance, when has anyone, anywhere asked them about anything – EVER. People mostly turn and run."

Eve laughed, "Well, I have to admit, whenever I run into someone who does anything with insurance, that's my response."

"And, if that doesn't work, I can always ask if they are adequately covered – always happy to take a look."

"You'll have them running faster than if they'd seen a ghost!" she choked out between laughs.

Michael led her down the spiral staircase and back into the apartment.

"I'm having such a great time, might there be a bit more champagne?"

"Actually, there's enough left in the bottle for two glasses." Michael poured what was left of the champagne into the glasses and handed one to Eve.

She walked to the sofa and sat toward one end. The sofa was soft and she began to melt into it. "Tell me more about the trip."

"Okay. River cruise down the Rhine. We embark in," he paused, picked up a piece of paper from a printer in the corner, and ran his finger down a paper, "Basel – in Switzerland. Before that, there will be two days in Lucerne. Then, seven days down the river to Amsterdam."

"Sounds like it will be a great adventure," Eve yawned. "Sorry. And, us?"

"We'll be a couple from the U. S., taking this opportunity to be together. We've been married a few years and we've been busy building our careers. This is a chance to reconnect."

"So, are we happy? I mean," she was having trouble

formulating what she wanted to say. Her arms and legs were like lead. Travel, fatigue, and the wine, no doubt, were all having their effect.

"Medium happy. We can't be gushing newlyweds and we can't be bickering. We don't want to stand out. When the job is finished, we want to be barely remembered. Just in case."

"So, just sort of there? Not happily married?" A slight hollowness appeared. Maybe it would be nice to actually have a home and family, something more than a career. "Wait. Just in case of what?"

Michael paused and looked at her. "Just in case somebody we don't want asking questions starts looking for who outed the congressman. And, I'm not sure 'happily married' exists in the real world."

"But John and Meg."

"They may be the exceptions. I'm sure the congressman puts on a happy face for his constituents, but he wouldn't be off on this – tryst, if he were. About half of marriages end in divorce. We're playing a part."

"Okay," but she wasn't quite sure she was at the moment. "Where are we from?"

Michael started to answer, but Eve was dissolving in a soft, warm fog. Words became fuzzy sounds and soon she had no desire to figure out the noises that were trying to pull her back to the world of the waking.

Michael stopped mid-sentence and smiled at her sleeping figure. He removed her shoes and carefully placed a pillow under her head. Then, he took a blanket from the bedroom and covered her. Before heading to the other room, he took one more look at the beautiful woman. *Happily married*, he thought. *It would be nice, but I know better from experience. Still.*

Eight

"Hello?"

"Hi, Meg. It's Eve."

"Eve! How was dinner?"

"And dinner was great. Really great! I spent the night."

"You slut! Saves your life, takes you to lunch, cooks dinner, and . . ."

"It wasn't like that. In fact, I'm a little embarrassed."

"You should be."

"Shush! My story. My story. He cooked a lovely dinner. We had champagne, then he took me to a roof garden on the top of his apartment, and we watched the sun set. You can see the Eiffel Tower from his roof."

"You did it on the roof!?"

"Meg, really. No afterward, we finished a bottle of champagne. I fell asleep on his couch."

"Okay, for the sake of propriety, you fell asleep. You didn't pass out."

She ignored Meg's latest. "Anyway, this morning, I woke up on his couch – fully clothed, before you have a chance to add anything. He fixed me breakfast then had me wear one of his robes while he took my things to have them pressed."

"And sprayed with see-through mist, so he can see – you know."

"If he wanted to see my 'you-know,' he could have done it last night while I was . . ."

"Asleep?"

"Yes, asleep.

"So, it is going well. Have you snooped around his apartment while he's out?"

"Meg! How could you even suggest . .?" Eve closed the closet door and checked under the bed – *Ah, storage boxes, probably couldn't get away with pulling those out.*

"And?"

"Okay. Maybe a little. The place is ultra clean. I was almost afraid to use the shower. Oh, and there's a locked cabinet in his closet."

"Which you found when you accidentally fell into the closet? Oh, no, you were looking for cleaning supplies."

"Shut up." Both women were laughing. "But I wonder what he keeps in there."

"Probably whips and chains and handcuffs. Eve, still there?"

Eve paused in her inspection of the dresser drawers, "I

was just thinking of whips and chains and handcuffs – that's all." Both women were laughing again. "But I wanted to tell you something, but I'm not sure I'm supposed to."

"Best friends. Besides, I'm not sure I like it when some guy you've just met wants you to keep secrets."

"Well, it has to do with an assignment. He wants me to help." Eve heard a key in the door and scooted out of the bedroom. "He's back. Almost caught!" She plopped into one of the dinette chairs and picked up a cup of coffee just as the door opened.

Michael entered carrying her slacks and sweater. "They were able to make them presentable in a short time," he said. "Who's on the phone?"

"I'm talking to Meg. Can I tell her anything about – you know?"

Michael made a 'May I?' gesture and reached for the phone. Eve handed it to him. He found the button he wanted and put them on speaker.

"Hi, Meg. Michael here."

"Hi, Michael. It's nice to, well, sort of meet you."

"You, as well."

"John is in the other room. Is it okay if I get him?"

"Of course."

A moment later, John joined the call. "Hi, Michael.

Good to hear your voice."

"Yours too, *mon ami*. I guess Eve wants to catch Meg up. In short, I'm supposed to do a story on a sleazy family values congressman who is currently vacationing with a very young lady who is not his wife. They're going to be on a river cruise, and I'd stick out like a sore thumb if I went alone. I've asked Eve to join me," Michael paused, "posing as my wife."

Eve sipped her coffee and listened to the conversation. *Am I really going to do this? Can I do this? It sounds dangerous and fun, but I'm not used to this. I'm more than a little scared. I don't have to decide right now, do I?*

"Undercover?" John asked.

"Superficially, yes. Eve can still be a designer for Eve-M fashions, and she can use her real name. That way, she doesn't have to learn a part."

"Who will you be?" It was Meg's voice.

"I'll be an insurance broker – maybe underwriter, named George Franklin.

"How will the story be handled?" It was John.

"They'll never know who got the information. I'll send the story along to the boss. They'll use some phony by-line. I'll make sure any pictures can't be traced to us."

"Eve is a good friend, Michael." It was John. "A really good friend." A warm wave poured through Eve. "She isn't used to this, and I'd hate to see any repercussions. Likely, this guy has backers. I'd like to add a layer."

"What did you have in mind, John?"

"Let's make her Evelyn Bellow – B-e-l-l-o-w. Pronunciation of her last name can stay the same. The business can be Evelyn B Couture. I'll have some cards made up and send them – where?"

"I think it's going to be the Schweizerhof in Lucerne."

"Okay, I'll take care of that. If you're careful, nobody will be the wiser. But if somebody does start looking, it will be nice to have a blind alley as protection. You might also see if she will change her hair color."

"What?" Now it was Eve's turn.

"Face it, Eve," said John, "You're gorgeous. Nobody could make you a frump, but it would be nice if you were a little more unrecognizable – just in case."

Eve wasn't sure she wanted to change her hair color, even for a short period of time, but hearing John say she was gorgeous made her tingle. But there was that 'just in case' thing again.

"Not to keep Eve out of the discussion, my vote is for brunette. Even with red hair, people will be walking into light posts, walls, etc."

"You're right, Michael. Brunette is probably the best choice. Eve, dear," John calling her dear made her perk up, "it is for the best. Michael, I'll get to work on the cards and stuff. I'll have them sent overnight to the hotel –

Schweizerhof? – to your attention – well, George Franklin."

"Nice talking to you, John," said Michael.

"You as well, Michael. Good luck. We should let the ladies get back to the private conversation we interrupted."

Both Eve and Meg took their phones off speaker.

"Well, Eve, it may be difficult for you to get your hair done. I mean your head must be really big after all the nice things both John and Michael said."

"Oh, did they? I wasn't listening." Both women laughed. "I guess I'd better figure out how I'm going to change my hair color. I don't know how hard it is to get an appointment, and I don't want to have it done in an alley. I have to confess, I'm a little scared. I've never done anything like this before. What if I screw up? What if I panic?"

"Don't worry," said Meg. "I'm sure you'll do fine, but you need to decide pretty soon. I'm also sure you'll look absolutely gorgeous." Both women continued to laugh, but Meg knew it would be hard to do anything that would make Eve look less than beautiful.

The women hung up. Michael was coming out of the bedroom. He was just hanging up his phone. He had a ring box in his hand. When he opened the box, there was a set of rings. The man's ring was a platinum band inset with diamonds – not chips, actual diamonds. The woman's engagement ring was a three-row pave engagement setting in platinum with a one carat cushion cut diamond. The wedding band, also platinum, had a single row of diamonds.

Eve gasped audibly. "Oh my god! That is absolutely gorgeous. Oh my god!" After a minute, she said, "This is just a prop, right? These aren't real."

"Well, we sometimes have to go places where people will know the difference. These are real. But they've never been worn by anyone else. You're the first."

"How much, I mean, I'm not sure I should be wearing . . ."

"A lady should never ask how much was spent on her engagement ring," he said with a smile. "May I?"

She watched as he took the ring out of the box and slid it onto her finger. It was a perfect fit. "I always thought that when this happened, my Prince Charming would be kneeling." Eve regretted the words when they came out of her mouth. She didn't want to sound pushy or demanding. She knew Michael still had wounds.

Almost before he knew what he was saying, he replied, "And when it is for real, I" he paused, "he will be." Then, hurriedly, he said, "In public, we have to act as if we are married."

Eve interrupted, "You mean I have to complain that you don't pay enough attention to me and you have to tell me it is because I am getting fat and I'm unappealing."

Michael stopped, stared, and started laughing hysterically. "I can't imagine that happening." And he kissed her. Not a long or passionate kiss, but her knees went a bit weak. And a warm, happy feeling poured through her body.

Something like warm cocoa on a winter morning – along with a tingling in her fingers and toes. *"I know it isn't real, but wouldn't it be nice? Even pretend feels nice."*

Eve took the man's ring from the ring box. She asked, "Do you mind if I pretend?"

"No. Go ahead."

She placed the ring on Michael's finger and said, "With this ring, I thee wed." And she kissed him.

The both stood, blushing, and Eve said, "Thank you." Then, both turned and stumbled around the apartment aimlessly, not quite knowing what to do next.

"Oh," said Michael, "I got you an appointment to get your hair done. It's okay. I know them. They'll do a good job."

Eve thought, *I hope so. How much can a man know about how to do a woman's hair – or how particular she is?*

Nine

She was very pleasantly surprised by the quality of the salon he had arranged. The staff were friendly and professional, and knew what they were doing. She was treated like royalty and wondered how Michael knew about this place. While she was having her hair done, Eve also received a manicure and pedicure. When she looked at the clock, she still had some time. *I could also work in a thirty-minute massage. How much could it cost, anyway?* After she was done, she was served a light lunch and a glass of champagne. She cringed, thinking Meg would never forgive her for the expense, but then, what better way to investigate – that's right, investigate – Paris fashion.

Completely relaxed and refreshed, Eve went to the counter and asked for the 'addition,' or bill.

"That has already been taken care of, Madame. Monsieur Thomas has paid the bill – and *pour boir* – how you say – gratuity. You are very lucky to have such a generous friend."

When Michael picked her up, she said, "You didn't have to pay for that. I was perfectly willing . . ."

"I know, but it is the least I could do. You're helping me out, and to do that, you had to," he paused, looking for the right words.

"Yes, I had to put up with a luxurious morning in a Paris salon. How will I ever recover." The both laughed.

"By the way," he said, "you still look stunning."

There's that warm, tingly feeling again.

They spent the afternoon and evening together. Eve checked out of her hotel and took her bags to Michael's. They had dinner in a small café around the corner and headed home fairly early.

"I can take the couch," he said. "You take the bed."

"You can't sleep on the couch. You'll end up with aches and pains you don't deserve."

"What do you suggest, Mademoiselle?"

"First, it is madame, not mademoiselle." she said, holding up her hand and smiling, "We're married now. We can both stay dressed, well, in pajamas, and sleep in the same bed. I'll try not to snore or drool. And, I promise I'll be a good girl. You don't have to be afraid."

"Do all men find you irresistible?"

That warm tingly feeling returned. "I don't know. I only care about some men." And, she kissed him on the cheek.

They took their bathroom turns. Michael found two sets of pajamas. Eve decided for the occasion she wouldn't go commando. Michael turned off the lights and they each crawled onto their respective sides. She couldn't resist, "See, here we are. Just like real married people – no sex."

Ten

The next morning, Eve opened her eyes, slowly, not sure at first where she was. Reality returned. She was snuggled next to Michael who was on his back. Her arm was over his chest and her right leg over his. She knew she should disengage, but she didn't want to wake him. Besides, she was warm, safe, and satisfied where she was. Slowly, she started to remove her arm.

"You can stay there a little longer, if you wish. I won't complain," he whispered.

First, she froze, then relaxed. "How long have you been awake?"

"Maybe twenty minutes. You seemed so relaxed and happy, I didn't have the heart to move."

"I'm sorry."

"No need to be sorry," he said, "I enjoyed your being near me as much as you did."

"I doubt that," she thought with a smile.

They finally got up. He fixed eggs, bacon, toast, and fruit for breakfast. As Eve ate, he showered and dressed, reappearing as she finished.

"That was exquisite!" she said. "You're going to make me fat."

"I doubt that. But, thank you. Why don't you get ready, and I'll tidy up?"

When she came out, ready to go, the apartment was again immaculate. They grabbed their bags and called a taxi, which Michael seemed to be able to get without trouble.

They arrived at Gare de Lyon before 10 in the morning. Built for the 1900 Paris Exposition, Eve was fascinated by the ornate architecture. She was amazed at how well the train system worked in Europe. They were neat, clean, and ran on time. The train they wanted didn't have any seats in second class.

"Well," said Michael, "let's see what we can do." He walked to the kiosk and returned a few minutes later. "There. All better."

"These are Premiere tickets," she said. "Aren't these expensive? I don't know if I can – or should get used to Premiere treatment."

"The company is paying the bill. Enjoy the part you are playing. They appreciate your participation – almost as much as I do."

She smiled. "*almost as much as I do,*" ran through her mind. "*This just might turn out better than a riverboat adventure. And that, would be lovely.*"

They walked down the platform and boarded the train. The Premiere car was elegant. As expected, it was not filled to capacity. The train left on time. The TGV (*Train à Grande Vitesse*) was a high-speed train, traveling at up to 200 miles per hour. The landscape flew past.

"So," she said, "tell me about this assignment and what I'm supposed – and maybe more importantly – NOT supposed to do."

"Well, first of all, you can be comfortable with being a fashion designer. That shouldn't pose a problem. I think John will have made up cards and done a business creation – just in case, so Evelyn B Couture will look legitimate. The hardest part will be pretending to be married to me," he said with a smile. "We won't be sure just what opportunities will come up, or how, so we'll play it by ear. I'll do my best to guide you. One thing, though, we don't' want to overdo it."

"Overdo it?"

"Yes. We can't be hanging on them. Unless there is a specific reason, every other day is probably enough contact. Oh, and we can arrange the sleeping arrangements to your satisfaction. If you'd like, I can crash on the floor. I've slept in worse places."

"Don't be silly – silly. You're not going to sleep on the floor. We'll figure something out."

The train left Paris, and soon they were riding through the French countryside. "*In a way*, she thought, *this could be anywhere in the U. S. – farms, villages.*" Then, they would pass a village with a castle ruin or a church that looked to have been built hundreds of years ago. A waiter in black trousers and jacket delivered flutes of champagne and porcelain plates containing pieces of fresh baguette and a variety of cheeses. She turned her head to look at Michael, smiled and said, "I wonder what the common people are doing." They both laughed.

The TGV arrived in Basel. They caught a local train to Lucerne and a taxi for the short ride to the hotel.

The Schweizerhof was built in the 1840s, and the lobby still had the old world feel of Neo-Renaissance. Eve loved it. From the marble columns to the ornate ceilings, the hotel was everything she could imagine in a fine world-class experience.

"This is absolutely beautiful! I love that the Europeans respect their past and heritage. It's like a trip to the past!"

"Yes, Anastasia once stayed in this hotel."

"You mean . . .?"

"Yes, THAT Anastasia."

The hotel staff were friendly and professional. As they checked in, Michael and Eve, now George and Evelyn, were told that the room had been paid, but were asked for a credit card for incidentals. Michael handed over a card.

"Thank you, Mr. Franklin. I hope you have a nice stay. The bus for the river cruise will leave at noon tomorrow. Oh, yes, this package arrived for you from the U.S. this morning." The desk clerk handed Michael an eight by ten envelope.

"So," began Eve when they were in the elevator alone, "why didn't they ask you why George Franklin was using Michael Thomas' credit card?"

Michael handed her the card, and she saw the name George Franklin on the front.

"How . . .?"

"Easy enough. When I got the assignment, things were taken care of. Like this card, the reservation on the cruise, things like that."

While the lobby was filled with old world charm, they found the rooms to be updated and modern. The bath was modern, as well, with a shower you could almost drown in. Three shower heads sprayed her while one overhead was like a heavy rain. Eve was fascinated. She was even more fascinated that Michael seemed to take all of this as routine.

"How can you seem so, I don't know, ho-hum about this beautiful room and hotel? Look at that view – Lake Lucerne right out our window."

"I guess I'm thinking about the assignment. You're right, it is very nice – especially the view. I really like the way it makes you happy."

"Well, no matter what happens, this alone has made it all worthwhile. Dinner, champagne, sunset over Paris, a spa day. Wow! Oh, yes, I almost forgot, you probably saved my life, too."

"I can't think of a life more worth saving. And you have been a delight."

The warm tingles returned when he said she was a delight. Most of the guys who, frankly, hit on her weren't anything like this man. And he hadn't tried to take advantage of any of the opportunities he'd had.

They had a little time before dinner, so Michael opened the package from John. Inside were 50 business cards for Evelyn B Couture, complete with phone number, e-mail address, and web site. The cards were chic and professional. In addition, were business cards for George Franklin, underwriter for Universal Casualty Company."

"I see I'm in San Francisco. Good address?"

"Good, yes. Perfect, no. This way, you look successful, but we didn't want you to be in New York. It would be too easy to check on you. The congressman is from the south, so it is unlikely he is familiar with San Francisco. Probably would have been better to have you from Toronto, but that would have posed some logistical problems we just didn't have time for."

"And the e-mail and website?"

"I'm sure John got the website up and running. Probably has some phony fashions posted."

Michael pulled out five thin catalogs from the envelope. "Oh, not that you'll be passing these out, but if need be, here are some catalogs – your fall line."

"You don't miss anything. How long did all this take?"

"Not much longer than half a day in the salon," he said with a smile.

Dinner in the hotel was prohibitive – more than $250

for a relatively spare meal. Add $100 if you want wine. Around the corner, the restaurant Gelateria dell' Alpi was excellent and significantly less expensive.

Back at the hotel, it was time, again, for bed. Back in pajamas, they slipped into bed on their separate sides.

Just before lights out, Eve said, "This is all so wonderful. The funny thing is, I'm not sure if any of this would have happened without the article written in Fashion Week. That's what started it all off. And wonderful things have happened ever since."

Michael was looking at her strangely. Then, he turned off the lights and they went to sleep.

Eleven

They took their time getting up and ready the following morning. They decided to forego the sponsored walking tour of Lucerne, although Eve thought it might be fun. Instead, they had a leisurely breakfast and made sure everything was packed. Real pieces of identification were locked securely away, "just in case," Michael had said.

With a bit of time to spare, Michael asked if Eve would like walk to the Chapel Bridge.

"It will give us time to chat about our cruise and the parts we'll play."

They walked out the front of the hotel and along the lake. There was a Movenpick ice cream kiosk, and Michael asked if she had ever had any. When she said, "No," he said she had to try some. She opted for cherry vanilla. Michael picked Swiss chocolate.

"Oh, my God!" she said, "I've never had anything this good. What's in it? Narcotics?"

"Shush!" he said, laughing. "You'll get us arrested. It is just much better than the stuff they pawn off on unsuspecting Americans in the States."

"This alone is worth moving to Europe for."

"It is really the ice cream I keep the job for," he said. "If it weren't for this, I would have returned years ago."

Eve found she was having a wonderful time with this man she'd just met.

It was a short walk to the bridge.

"Kapellbrücke literally means chapel bridge. It was built in the 1300's and is the oldest remaining wooden covered bridge in Europe. They say it was used by soldiers to cross back and forth across the river."

Their footfalls on the old wood echoed in the semi-enclosed space. On the other side of the railing the river quietly rolled quickly on. The wood was worn and weathered, and for some reason Eve relaxed and felt very much at home. A breeze through the bridge gave her a quick chill, and she pulled closer to Michael.

"This is beautiful," she said. "What are the paintings – there on the . . .?"

"Trusses. They were done in support of the church – Catholic Church, during the counter reformation."

They paused to allow a large group of tourists pass.

"And that tower?" she asked pointing to the single octagonal stone fortification rising out of the water next to the bridge.

"It's known as the water tower – not to hold water, but – you know – a tower in the water. Originally, it was of military importance – a prison, a place to torture prisoners. Later, it was used as an archive. A different kind of torture, if you will." The last he said with a smile.

She sighed and shrugged at the lame joke. "Why don't you take this time to tell me more about our parts."

"Okay. You and me. We've been married a little over three years. We both know what our professions are. We've worked hard for the time we've been married, and we've decided that we needed to take time to reconnect. Our lives together are more important than work."

"Our first marriages?" she asked. "We're a little older than a lot of, well, kind of newlyweds."

"Yes, our first. For both of us. No need to complicate the backstory with former marriages, divorces, kids, all that. Then, too, someone always asks what the former – spouse – was like. It's just simpler this way."

"Are we trying to start a family on this trip, you know, have children?"

He turned and looked at her, stared at her for a good minute. His face had no expression. She found it unsettling. Finally, he said, "No. No children. We're just trying to reconnect." He turned away from her and almost under his breath said, "No children."

Eve felt the chill return and she was suddenly very much alone. She walked to the railing, watching the water pass by the bridge. Michael didn't follow.

Michael was quiet. Finally, he escorted her to the hotel. In their room, they made sure everything was in order. Michael checked Eve's things after she had them ready.

Just before it was time for them to meet the bus, he turned and said, "Ready?"

"I'm ready. Are you okay? You seem – distracted."

"I'm okay. It'll pass," he said without emotion.

They left their room and headed to the lobby in silence.

Twelve

Michael dropped their bags in the lobby where the Lucerne representative indicated. They would be loaded on the bus designated for them – for the drive, as it turned out, back to Basel to board the river boat.

They walked side by side around to the back of the hotel to board the bus. The sun was shining, and the day was warm. Eve was wearing khaki slacks, a long-sleeved white blouse, and a pair of women's casual fashion boat shoes. She carried a white V-neck button cardigan in the event the air conditioning on the bus made for a cold ride. Michael was in charcoal slacks and a solid short-sleeved shirt. He stopped just outside the door to allow Eve to climb the stairs first, then he followed. Passengers had taken many of the front seats, so Michael gestured toward the back of the bus. Eve sat by the window, Michael on the aisle. Some of the passengers were talking, many were silent.

Eve turned to Michael, "Can you tell me what it was . . .?"

He looked at her, his eyes sad. "I'm sorry. I'll explain some time, but the explanation – if I do it now – will take too long and will interfere with what we need to do. I'm sorry, but please try to understand. We need to concentrate on the job."

She wasn't sure. Something she'd said about children had caused his response, she couldn't figure out what it was. *What would happen if someone on the trip said something similar? And, what was it about children? Meg knew. If only Meg had told her – maybe she could have avoided this.*

About fifteen minutes late, the last of the stragglers had been rounded up and loaded on the bus. A couple from Indiana. She'd had to go into one last, or was it two last, shops to find something she thought would be perfect. The door closed, and the bus headed out. The air conditioning came on, and Eve, glad she'd brought the sweater, put it on.

It didn't take long to leave the city. One of the river boat's crew gave a running monolog about the cruise. Eve supposed it was to take everyone's mind off the nondescript countryside that was sliding past the windows.

After an hour and a half, the bus came to a stop and people started to get out of their seats, stretch, and head for the door. Michael was slow to rise. Finally, when just about everyone was off the bus, he started to get up. He turned to her and said, "This is it. Show time. No dress rehearsal. If you don't want to do it, let me know now. We can figure something out to get you out of it. Otherwise, Mrs. Evelyn Bellow, the curtain is about to rise."

"Of course, I want to do it. Why do you ask?"

"Sometimes, like jumping out of an airplane, things are much more appealing when you talk about them – not so much when it comes time to perform."

"By the time we're done, you won't believe how well I perform," she said with a smile and lightness she wasn't sure she felt. *But I guess I'm really doing this*, and she looked to heaven and asked that she not mess up.

"That's my girl. Thank you," he said with a smile. Then, he led her down the aisle to the front of the bus, down the stairs, and back out into the sun.

She was almost stunned when she saw where they were. The bus was on the side of the road, next to a small park. On the other side of the park was a sidewalk, then, the river – the Rhine, she'd been told. A beautiful long ship was tied up, and a gangway was placed from the sidewalk to the side of the ship.

When Michael had said a riverboat cruise, she had visions of paddle wheelers that plied the Mississippi River. This ship was long, she guessed over four hundred feet, low, she could see onto the top of the ship from where she was standing, and sleek. It was a beautiful and modern ship. Michael had to pull on her arm to start her toward the ship she was so mesmerized. They walked across the park and the sidewalk, then started down the gangway.

The gangway was placed so they would enter the side of the ship on the first, later what they learned as the middle, level, near the center of the ship. The first person to greet them was the cruise director, whose name was Nick. He handed them off to another crew member who checked to make sure they were the right passengers. "You'd be amazed how many people try to stow away," he said laughing. They were each handed a glass of champagne and given keys to their room. The crewman led them down the passage to their room, made sure the keys worked, and checked to make sure the room was acceptable.

The crewman pointed to what looked like an

electronic door lock fastened to the wall. "Like most hotels in Europe now, one of the room keys must be inserted into this device to make the lights and outlets work. Our little way of saving electricity when you are out of the room. When you take your key, all electricity is cut off." He told them there was a briefing in the lounge, forward and one deck up, in thirty minutes. Their luggage would be delivered during the briefing.

The crewman left, and the door closed.

"Wow!" said Eve. "I can't get over . . . I mean, I feel like royalty."

"I'm impressed," said Michael. "They really seem to know what they are doing."

They set about exploring their cabin. It wasn't large, but there was everything they would need, including a full and private toilette, with shower. The bed was a queen size.

"If you'd like to sleep on the side nearest the bathroom, I can find a place on the floor, here near the sliding glass door."

"Don't be ridiculous," said Eve. "We're adults. We'll share the bed. And, like all reasonable married couples, if we have an argument, you can sleep on the couch." Then, they both laughed.

"But, Madame, there is no couch."

"In that case, sir, I would advise you to avoid any disagreements."

The tension between them vanished, and about that time, the chimes sounded and an announcement was made for passengers to gather in the lounge. Eve had moved to the sliding door that exited to the room's small balcony. At the sound of the chimes, she started to move toward the door. Michael was standing at the foot of the bed, and their bodies brushed as she moved past. There was a swirling in Eve's belly. She turned to apologize, but their eyes met and neither said anything. Eve's swirling turned to a heat, spreading within her. Suddenly, her face was hot.

"Uh, I'm, uh," Eve's hand was making a disconnected gesture. *What am I, in junior high?* she thought.

"Yeah. We should, um, head up to the – the meeting."

They left their room, and he took her hand. They walked forward. The passageway was narrow. A plush blue carpet padded their feet. They walked across the reception area and were guided up the stairs to the lounge – a large room with plenty of seating. The walls between the lounge and outside world were glass floor to ceiling, giving a magnificent view.

This is incredible, thought Eve. *It's like we're in a sophisticated lounge in some exotic setting.* Michael chose a seat toward the front of the ship, on one side. The seat faced backwards, which made seeing the speaker difficult unless they twisted in their seats.

"Wouldn't it be better . . ." she started to ask

Michael leaned over and nuzzled her ear. "I want to see who comes in. We need to find our – you know."

Eve was having so much fun she had almost forgotten the reason for this trip, but feeling Michael nuzzle her ear made her hair stand on end with sensual desire.

A woman in uniform started talking. She welcomed them to the cruise and explained that the staff was split into two distinct parts. The first, ran the ship, and consisted of five men: the captain, the first officer, the engineer, and two hands. The second ran what she called the ship's hotel, and there were forty-nine. She ran through the basic functions of the people on board, then introduced the captain.

"Welcome to you all. We have only five crew to run the boat, so while we will see you from time to time, mostly we will be working to get you to where you want to be without delay. One request we always seem to have is tours of the command center – the ship's bridge – only on this ship, it is so much more. We will schedule a time for you to visit when the workload is less. You may notice that our command center goes up and down – up to a height of nine meters when we want to see farther, it also drops almost flush with the deck so we can pass under bridges when the river is high. Are there any questions?"

From a woman in the back of the lounge, "Why aren't there any lifeboats on board?"

"Well," the captain explained, "when we travel the river, most of the time we will be within six feet of the bottom. If the ship were to sink – and that hasn't happened yet," he said smiling, "the ship will settle on the bottom and everyone will be escorted to the sun deck where they will be served complimentary champagne until we are rescued."

With that, the hotel manager returned and introduced the cruise director. There was a quick overview of the activities for the rest of the day, and the meeting ended.

Michael got up and went to the bar. He returned with two glasses of champagne. "Our friend and his friend didn't attend. I hope this doesn't mean we're on the wrong ship. Gives the original meaning back to missing the boat."

"They probably stayed in their cabin – er, stateroom," countered Eve.

"I hope. I'd hate to think this might be a wasted effort."

"How can you say this is a wasted effort? I might feel offended."

"Oh, God! I'm sorry. I didn't mean. I'm sorry."

She started to laugh. "I'm not sure that makes up for the wine out the nose, but the look on your face was priceless."

After their champagne, they headed downstairs to dinner. They had their choice of fried white fish or chicken. Both looked excellent. Eve opted for the fish. Michael for the chicken. White wine was served. Both entrees were done to perfection, and Michael and Eve swapped bites of theirs.

Halfway through dinner, Michael nudged her with his foot. When she looked at him, he nodded slowly toward the entrance. Just entering was a middle-aged heavyset man and a young woman. Eve gasped. Luckily, they were at a table alone.

"He's old enough to be her father!" she whispered.

"Shush!" he whispered. "Now you know why. Back home he runs on a family values platform. Back home, he has a wife and almost grown children."

She put her napkin to her mouth to quiet the sound even more. "I have to wonder if that girl isn't the same age as his kids. Or younger."

"Well, it's a good thing it happened this way. Now you won't have a shocked reaction when we run into them later. Will you?"

"No, I'll be . . . how do you know we'll run into them later?"

"Because that's why we're here. That's the job."

They passed on dessert and headed back to the stateroom.

"We'll have to see what times they go to meals. We'll try to start there. If we can sit with them at meals, we can strike up a conversation – whatever seems interesting."

"Like what flavor bubble gum is popular in junior high school?" she asked.

"We'll try for something a bit more sophisticated than that. The young lady might have an interest in fashion, for example." He turned the key and opened the door. They entered and turned on the light. On what served as a dresser was a bottle of champagne – Moet and Chandon. Michael opened the accompanying envelope. He gave out a soft chuckle and shook his head.

"What?" asked Eve.

He handed her the card. It said, *Best Wishes, SJ*.

"Who's 'SJ?'

"We just call him Saint Jude. The boss nobody has ever met. He's the one responsible for saving us, us Digbys, if that's what you want to call it."

"Why Saint Jude? Is he Catholic?"

"Don't know about his religion, but St. Jude is the patron saint of lost causes. That's what we are."

She looked at Michael, then at the card, then at Michael. Then, she went to him and gave him a hug. "You're not a lost cause."

"Well, each of us – at least the ones I know about – has come to some sort of a dead end in life. Then, voila, it's like another chance. Not a complete do over, but a place to be while life sorts itself out."

"And your dead end?"

"Let's just leave it as I had a bad experience once."

"It must have been really bad. A woman?"

"Just – just leave it. Concentrate on the job."

Thirteen

Eve looked at the only light she could see; clock in the stateroom. It was after one in the morning, but not quite two. She had been awake for some time. She wasn't sure how long. Her mind was spinning. It started with the congressman and the young girl – Eve hadn't seen her up close, yet, but she wondered if the girl was even of legal age. And, how any young woman's parents could agree to this. Or, was it essentially kidnapping? That set of depressing thoughts melted into the river cruise. It was a wonderful experience. At least without the thought of why they were there. Well, why they were tasked with being there. Finally, she thought back to the way Michael had responded when she had asked a simple question about whether, in their pretend parts, they should say they were trying to start a family. There had to be something about children, or about starting a family, that was part of his dark past – the one that seems to haunt every man who becomes the writer known to the world as Digby. Then, there was the comment he'd made before bed. She hadn't wanted to pry, well, maybe it was more she probably shouldn't have pried, but she wanted to know. She needed to know. When their bodies had touched after they'd come on board, there may not have been a fire, but something started to smolder.

Deciding she wouldn't sleep for a while, she slipped quietly out of bed and pulled on a set of dark slacks and a stylish pink sweater she'd picked up in Lucerne. She carried her deck shoes and left the stateroom as quietly as she could. Closing the door with a barely audible click, Eve slipped on her shoes and headed up the passageway toward the front of the ship.

One of the staff, a young brunette woman, was sitting at the reception desk in the atrium at the center of the ship. "Good evening ma'am. Couldn't sleep?"

"Um, no. I guess it is just almost too much to take in – the ship, the river. You know."

"Yes, it is exciting. Is there anything I can get for you?"

"Thank you, no. I'll just go upstairs for some air."

"Well, we'll be passing through some locks shortly," and the woman returned to her work.

Earlier in the day, Michael and Eve were on the sun deck, the uppermost deck of the ship, when they'd passed through a couple of locks. The ship had pulled into the lock and the gate closed behind them. Then, the entire level of water dropped, and the ship exited the front of the lock, some twenty feet lower on the river. It was fascinating to experience the ship sinking lower and lower into the lock, as the walls appeared to grow higher and higher.

Eve climbed the stairs at the front of the reception area. The lounge was dark. A small library ringed the back of the atrium on this deck. She exited the interior and took an exterior stairway onto the sundeck. She walked halfway from the middle of the ship to the stern. The night was cool, and she was glad she'd decided on a sweater. The moon was up, behind the ship, illuminating the landscape. They were just passing the last part of a small town that hugged the river. Few lights were on, and Eve surmised the town was asleep, as well. The night was soundless and there was almost no sensation of motion.

At the edge of the town she spotted the dark outline of an old church. She wasn't an expert in architecture, but in the moonlight, she guessed it might date from Medieval times. She thought about the people who might have built it and the generations of those who'd attended services there. What history the church would have seen!

Behind Eve, soundlessly, the small ship's command center began to withdraw – lower – into the ship. She thought about sitting in one of the deck chairs, and looked around for one. The shrinking ship's bridge caught her eye momentarily. Then she returned to looking at the small town receding on the riverbank and wondering what life was like there.

Unseen by her, a vehicle crossing bridge ahead extended across the river at the lock and would pass barely four feet over the deck missing the ship's command center by inches.

Fourteen

In the stateroom, Michael rolled over and his arm slid onto what was Eve's side of the bed. Slightly roused by finding her gone, he quietly called out her name. When there was no response, he sat up, turned, and put his feet on the floor. He called her name, again. Again, there was no response. He reached to the window curtains. A quick look told him she wasn't on the small balcony. He stood and picked up a small flashlight he'd placed on the nightstand. He walked to the door, turned, and noted the bathroom door was open and no one was inside.

Michael pulled on a pair of shorts and a pair of canvas slip-ons. He made sure to put a key into his pocket, noting that the second key was still in the electrical device.

"She won't be able to get back in the room," he thought, *"without her key. I'll need to remind her."* Outside the room, there was only one way to go, so, he headed forward. In the few minutes since Eve had passed, the shift had changed. The young man now sitting in reception said he hadn't seen her. The restaurant on the second level was obviously closed, so he headed to the third level. The lounge was dark, and the small library was empty. At the front of the atrium was a coffee service and muffins. He reminded himself to pick up one of each after he'd found Eve.

Michael exited the ship and walked to the stern outside, instead of taking the stairs at the atrium, as Eve had. The night was cool, and there was a slight breeze. He'd have to come back and do this cruise for pure fun someday, he thought. At the stern of the ship, he climbed the stairs still heading aft, then, at the top of the ladder, he turned to face forward.

He saw her, bathed in moonlight, hair moving in the light breeze. She was oblivious to everything, studying something far behind on the riverbank, looking beautiful. Out of the corner of his eye, he caught movement. At the bow, there was something big and black. It spanned the channel and was at least ten feet high. It was moving down the ship, he knew it had to be a bridge the ship was passing under.

"Eve!" he cried, but she was lost in reverie.

"Eve!" again, he cried. She began to look around, confused at the sound of her name.

He started to run toward her, his gaze shifting between her and the looming bridge. "Eve! Down!" he yelled, but she didn't understand. She stood looking at him.

He was moving as fast as he could, but his feet just slipped on the dew-covered surface. He slammed to one knee. Pain shot through his leg. "The bridge!" He clawed at the deck with his hands. He was pushing with his feet, his knees. The bridge was closer. "Eve! Down!" He'd never make it in time. Then, Eve, looking confused, started to walk toward him.

Yes! Yes! he thought. *Come on!* Then, she stretched out her arm to reach him. He grabbed her wrist and yanked. She fell on top of him. Her weight crushed him to the deck, knocking the wind out of him. He gasped, trying to suck air into his lungs.

"What the . . .?" she started to say, then the moonlight disappeared. The bridge passed over the boat, not three feet above their heads.

He felt her start to shake. "That could have . . ."

His voice was weak. There wasn't enough air in his lungs yet. "Yes, but it didn't. Are you okay?" When she didn't answer, he asked again, "Are you okay?"

"I was just, um, ah – yes, I'm – okay," she finally answered.

He put his arms around her. "God! I don't know what I would have done." There were tears in his eyes.

Just then, one of the crew ran up. "Are you two okay? We usually check up here before every bridge transition, but we didn't see anyone, and since it was two in the morning," the crew member let the sentence trail off.

"We're okay," said Michael. "We'd prefer that nobody make a big deal of this. Could we just forget it? There were no injuries or . . ."

The crewman looked relieved. "Yes, sir. Whatever you wish."

"Do you suppose we could sneak a couple of brandys out of the bar?"

"Yes. Sir. Why don't I bring them to your stateroom?"

Five minutes later, Michael thanked the crewman and closed the door, a bottle of brandy and two glasses in his hand. He gave a glass to Eve.

She was still rattled. Michael saw the glass shaking in her hand. "I could have been . . ."

"Yes, but you weren't." He took the glass and set it on the cabinet. "And I don't have to explain to your best friend how you were knocked off the boat by a moving bridge."

They turned off the lights and crawled into bed. She rolled against him and pulled his arm around her.

"What made you come after me?" she asked.

"I rolled over and you weren't in bed. A quick check showed you weren't in the room."

"I couldn't sleep. Too many things running through my mind. I thought a walk might settle me. I didn't want to disturb you. I tried to leave quietly."

"When I did a quick check, I saw you hadn't taken your key. If I'd been sound asleep, you couldn't have gotten back in without waking half the boat."

"So, if I HAD taken the key?" The thought hung in the air while both Michael and Eve thought about how differently the night might have ended if she had remembered the key. "By the way, thank you for saving my life."

"Your life was worth saving. I'm just glad . . ." He let the thought hang, but he thought, *"She should just be part of the job, but you're lying to yourself, Michael, if you tell yourself that."*

Fifteen

Eve awoke in a soft darkness. She could see by light coming through a small gap in the curtain that the sun was up. She rolled over and discovered Michael wasn't in bed. She stretched, turned her body parts in various directions, then sat on the edge of the bed. She rubbed her eyes with her hands, then stood and walked around the bed to the curtains covering the full-length sliding glass door to their very small balcony. She thought about yanking the curtains apart quickly to surprise herself with the new day, but the cruise director had warned against doing that.

"You never know where you'll be," he'd said. "One couple who like to sleep *au natural* yanked open their curtain to find they were tied up next to another ship, with a family in a stateroom six feet away."

She resisted the impulse and opened the curtain just far enough to see where they were. The ship had moored sometime during the night – well, early morning – and a few feet away was a park, with a walkway by the water. A young couple was walking their dog, looking at the ship, and a few people were sitting on the grass.

"Oops!" she said. "That could have been embarrassing." Then, she laughed at the thought of it. It might have given the folks in the park something to talk about later.

She found a note on the writing desk from Michael. He had gotten up early and was going to see if he could catch their quarry at breakfast. She dressed as quickly as she could, ran a brush through her hair, and headed for the restaurant.

Michael was seated at a table for eight on the left side of the restaurant, about halfway up. There were three other passengers at the table, in various stages of their meals. He was sipping a cup of coffee.

"There you are, dear," he said. "I was afraid you might miss breakfast, but I didn't want to wake you. You looked angelic while you were sleeping." He rose from his chair when she approached. He pulled back a chair for her and as she stepped in to take her seat, Michael kissed her.

She thought, "*A bit of play-acting for the passengers.*" But the kiss lasted two beats longer than she expected, and his hand slid from her side to her back. A tingle ran through her, and when their kiss ended, she kept Michael's gaze longer than she would have.

"Let me introduce you to these lovely people," started Michael. "This is Gordon Lovette and his wife Madge. Gordon sells restaurant equipment and Madge manages the homestead. They're here from St. Louis." Eve shook their hands and said, hello. "And this is Martha Vine. Martha is a retired teacher who lives in Pensacola, Florida." Again, Eve shook hands and passed pleasantries.

"We were just talking about the tour this morning," said Martha.

"Where are we? I guess one day on the ship and I've already lost track," said Eve.

"Breisach. Breisach, Germany," said Martha. "You must have slept pretty well, dear."

"Like I was practically knocked out," said Eve.

At that, Michael choked and started to cough up his coffee. He even managed to get some out his nose.

"Okay dear?" asked Eve, and when she looked at him, she winked in a way that only he could see. "Come. Come help me pick some things out from the breakfast buffet."

As they walked to the buffet, she turned and said, "I'm not sure I quite got you back for the wine out the nose in Paris, but it's a good start, don't you think?"

Michael took her hand and spun her around. Eve started to say "Wha . . .?" but her question was smothered by a long, passionate kiss that he placed on her lips. When the kiss ended, her legs were a little wobbly, and she was feeling a tingling energy building inside her.

"Wow!" she said. "What, why – I mean – was it the coffee thing, or . . ."

"You know you're beautiful."

"Are you kidding? I haven't showered, my make-up isn't right, I barely got a comb through my hair, and I just threw these on," she gestured at her clothes.

He kissed her again. This time, when their lips met, she ran her tongue across his lips. His lips parted, inviting her deeper. Heat flashed within her. It started in her stomach, but the heat flooded her. It was deep within her, a primal feeling. A primal need. She needed to stop. Now. Before she lost control of her response.

She broke with his mouth, turned her head away, startled by the heat that raged within her and afraid everyone would know what her body was doing. It took her a moment to focus. She noted the two women at the table they'd left were looking their way, trying to be nonchalant about it, but looking, just the same. Gordon was studying the pattern in the tablecloth.

"None of that matters," said Michael. "You are beautiful. So beautiful, I lost control, and I don't care. I'm lucky to have you with me, and," he paused. "And if anything had happened to you last night, I don't . . ."

"Nothing bad happened," she said huskily, searching for her normal voice. "And likely won't as long as I have my protector nearby. Now, let's get something to eat."

Michael had already eaten – more than he should have, he said. He wanted to be at breakfast early to figure out how to meet the congressman and his companion. Breakfast was almost finished, and they'd been a no-show. Eve was famished, but she took less than she really wanted. Michael took a few pieces of fruit.

They returned to the table and set down their plates. A waiter came by with two flutes of champagne. Eve thought that after seeing the two kisses, the waiter figured champagne was in order. Gordon had excused himself and was leaving the restaurant. Martha and Madge were still at the table, trying their best – and not succeeding very well –

to look like nothing out of the ordinary had happened.

"So, how long have you two been married?" asked Madge.

"Three years," answered Eve.

"Yes, three years," said Michael. "I've been so busy with work, I'm surprised she even puts up with me."

"She's doing fine," giggled Martha. "Just fine."

"We wanted to take this trip so that nothing would interfere with us being together," said Michael.

"So, does that mean you'll be trying to start a family?" asked Madge.

Eve braced herself. After Michael's reaction on the tour boat in Lucerne, she wasn't sure what was going to happen. She was starting to say that it was only a vacation, when Michael spoke up.

"Right now, we're just on vacation. Reconnecting. Who knows what might happen later, but right now, my mind is focused on enjoying the company of my beautiful wife."

Eve found that her mild panic at the question turned to a tingling feeling running through her body. She turned and looked at Michael, he was looking at her, a smile on his lips and in his eyes. The tingling feeling doubled.

Eve had a hard time focusing on her breakfast. She finally finished as announcements were being made for the tour of a part of the black forest.

As they made their way back to the stateroom, they passed couples headed the other way.

"We really need to make the tour. I need to get an idea of how to connect with them." Michael said the word 'them' in a way that left no doubt as to whom he meant.

Eve stopped at the stateroom door, turned to face Michael, and placed her hand on the door, extending her arm well above her head. "I want you to know, the kisses, the things you said – if you even half meant any of them, you might not be safe going into the stateroom alone with me."

His eyes met hers. She could see into his soul, and what she saw made the tingling – and the heat return within her. "I meant all that and more," he said, "and if you had any idea what I am thinking, you'd know you wouldn't be safe going into the stateroom alone with me. Unfortunately, we have a tour to catch. I can't remember when I've been . . ."

"Yeah. Me too."

Sixteen

They boarded the bus and headed for two unoccupied seats. Eve wore a white gathered neckline sleeveless sundress, a shell bracelet, and a pair of light green tassel boat shoes. She pulled a tube out of her bag, smiled, batted her eyes, and said, "I don't want to burn, would you be a doll and put some of this sunscreen on my back?"

Michael took the tube, squirted out a bit of sunscreen and warmed it in his hands before starting to rub it into Eve's shoulders. Because she had turned toward the window, Michael couldn't see the way her eyes rolled back into her head as he began to apply the sunscreen. A relaxing wave flowed down her arms to her tingling fingertips as he softly massaged the lotion into her shoulders. His soft touch pushed deeper as she relaxed and the muscles in her neck and upper back dissolved into a pool of relaxation. The more she relaxed, the more slowly and deeply he pushed. She could only imagine what would happen to her whole body if he continued.

"Uh, that's, I mean, I – think you've, um got it."

"Not yet," he said. "I want to make sure I don't miss a spot and I want to get enough rubbed in. I don't want to be the cause of your sunburn."

It took almost ten minutes for him to complete his task. Eve turned back, but she was a puddle. She was totally relaxed and warm. And she didn't care who knew. She sighed and leaned against Michael wondering what it might be like to have a longer, complete massage. She was breathing deeply, engrossed in a fantasy about a body-to-body, hot, sweaty, deep and prolonged massage. A deep sigh drained all the tension from her. While her back and shoulders were relaxed, deep inside, a hot desire was beginning to burn.

They held hands as the bus they were assigned to headed to the Black Forest. Their quarry was nowhere to be seen on their bus. They hoped for better luck with the other buses. Still, that meant they would only be able to connect during the tour itself.

They visited an outdoor museum where historic homes, some over four hundred years old, had been reassembled to look like a village of sorts. They learned to churn butter. And they stopped to have lunch. All the while, there was no sign of the congressman or the girl. As they walked through the attractions, they held hands. As they rode the bus, Eve kept her hand on Michael's mid-thigh. If she wanted to point something out, Eve would turn, point with one hand and slide the hand on his thigh back and forth, just a bit. And after the earlier sunscreen massage, she decided she needed to point a lot of things out.

"You're killing me here," he said.

"Oh, I'm sorry," she said sweetly. "Was it something I was doing?" Secretly, she was enjoying his sweet 'suffering.'

By the time they returned to the ship, it was ninety minutes before the afternoon briefing – the daily rundown of events for the night, the sailing schedule, and events for the next day. It had been a long half day. Both were hot, tired, and sweaty.

Eve put the key into the lock. "I'm really going to need to shower. I may take my time, so maybe you should go first." The door opened and the room had been made up. The sheer curtains were pulled closed across the sliding door to the balcony. The door closed behind Michael. They kicked off their shoes.

He took her by the hand and turned her around to face him. "I told you before that if you had any idea what I was thinking, you probably wouldn't feel safe with me alone in here. If you want me to stop, tell me to stop now. But if you don't . . ."

She stood on her toes and kissed him. Softly. Then, softly again. Then, they kissed more forcefully, their lips pushing together. Her tongue rubbed across his lips, then into his mouth. His tongue met hers. Her heart was pounding, her body was tingling. Something – pressure – was building within her. She was having trouble catching her breath. She felt his chest against hers. He was breathing hard and fast. He pulled her even closer. Their stomachs touched and his hardening cock pushed against her as their abdomens rubbed.

He picked her up and carried her the short distance to the bed. Her sundress came off in an instant. "I should shower," she started to say, but she was cut short by Michael's lips on hers. Then, he was kissing her neck and shoulders. She pulled at his shirt, frustrated because it was taking so long to remove. Then, she was fumbling with his shorts. She didn't care if she didn't seem sophisticated. Both of them were in heat, and nothing mattered. She finally got his shorts halfway down and started kissing his chest, the taste of salt on her lips. He pushed her back. He fumbled in the nightstand and pulled out a pouch. He ripped the pouch dumping the contents, among them, condoms. He fumbled with the package, finally ripping it apart. He put the rolled condom on the end of his rock-hard shaft and started to unroll it. Eve pushed his hand aside and gripped him, pushing her hand up his shaft, unrolling the condom as she went. Her breath was raspy.

He pulled at her briefs. He managed to get only one leg out. Eve started to reach to pull them off completely. She stopped halfway and sucked in her breath. His tongue had found its way between her legs. He was kissing and licking, then thrusting his tongue inside her. Over and over, she was twisting and turning, moaning, crying. His tongue was merciless. There was no thought. Nothing made sense. She wanted this energy, this pressure to release, to explode, but she didn't.

She grabbed him by the arms and pulled him. He advanced, licking, and kissing, and nipping his way up her body. She couldn't take any more. She pulled him within her. He pushed forcefully. She exhaled, then inhaled. She wanted him. She wanted him to drive into her as hard and as far as he could. Harder and harder. Deeper and deeper. "Yes!" That's what she wanted and that's what she was getting. Her arms were wrapped around him. She pulled him ever faster, her nails clawing into his back. Her legs were no longer her own. She was kicking and pushing and stretching. Now, she was groaning, almost snarling. Nothing mattered. She was lost in a world of tantalizing ecstasy.

All at once, everything stopped. He was still driving into her, but time, motion, and emotion almost ceased to exist. She lifted herself off the bed on her shoulders and heels, not even knowing she was doing it. She froze, and five seconds later, her orgasm detonated. Then, she imploded. Arms and legs contracting inward, her back curled, her head pulled forward. And the shaking started. Violently and uncontrollably. Michael, completely lost in his world, drove into her twice more before her contracting canal caused his explosion. They lay together, shaking. Slowly, they started to recover. Realization of where they were, what they had experienced.

Seventeen

Eventually, consciousness returned.

"Are you okay?" he asked.

Eve started to speak, but nothing came out. She cleared her throat. "Okay? Um, yeah, I'd say okay – if you're into understatements." They laughed. "I should have showered first," she said.

"Like I could have waited for a shower."

"What if – what if when you said – you know – if I didn't want to, I should have told you to stop? Would you have stopped?"

"I would have had to find a way. I probably would have shot myself."

Eve looked shocked – "Shot yourself?"

"But the way I was feeling, even that might not have stopped me." Then, they were both laughing.

"I suppose we should get cleaned up. Otherwise, EVERYONE will know how we spent the afternoon," she said.

"I don't really care. I don't think I've ever had an afternoon – wait a minute, that only took thirty minutes. Wow!"

"Wow! Is right. Still, I need to shower. A lady must look presentable. And the daily briefing is in an hour."

Eve showered first. The hot water caressed her body. *I'm completely worn out and relaxed – inside and out.* She thought about what had happened. She'd had sex before, *but I've never lost control, feeling like an animal in heat. Should I worry about that?* She smiled. *God, no! I can't wait for that to happen again*!

Michael showered second and only took a few minutes. When he left the bathroom, Eve was wearing a ship's robe, her hair still wrapped in a towel. She turned to look at him, one leg completely exposed. She saw his erection growing and pushing outside his robe.

"Really!? Do you think we have time for that? Ship's briefing in thirty minutes."

He answered by dropping his robe and pulling her up to him.

"What the hell," she said. His hard cock pushed against her. Heat built within her again as he pulled the robe open and pushed it from around her. The soft robe caressed her skin as it slid off her shoulders and fell to the floor. She felt his nakedness against hers. "Even if we're late, nobody will miss us," she finished as she crushed her mouth against his.

They managed to satisfy each other a little slower and softer than the first time. And then, by rushing to dress and ready themselves afterward, they managed to make it to the daily briefing just as it started.

"Good afternoon," said the cruise director. "I hope everyone had a great first day." Eve looked at Michael and squeezed his hand. "From time to time," continued the cruise director, "we will award prizes for things that happen during the course of the cruise. Because we don't know what might happen that deserves an award, we don't have the same awards for each trip."

"Today," he continued, "we have a prize that we haven't ever awarded before. George and Evelyn. George Franklin! Evelyn Bellow! Get up here!"

"Oh, crap," said Michael quietly. Eve just had a puzzled look on her face. Slowly they stood and started to walk to where the cruise director stood with the microphone.

"We've never awarded this prize before, so you're the first. You receive a bottle of Moet and Chandon as the prize for the best, most passionate kiss during the breakfast meal on board. Let's give them a hand folks! This is the kind of spirit we like to see. By the way," he continued, "you returned from the tour almost two hours before this briefing. After the kiss – kisses, I should say, at breakfast, would you like to tell us if you deserve another prize for anything that might have transpired between the tour end and this briefing."

Michael and Eve both blushed and were both so bright red there was no way to hide it.

At the cruise director's encouragement, the lounge erupted in applause.

"Thank you, folks. I hope we haven't embarrassed you

completely."

The rest of the briefing went off routinely. Dinner followed directly after. They were able to spot the congressman, but by the time they headed toward that table, it had filled.

Their tablemates were friendly. They got a bit of ribbing about their award. Eve told Michael later that two of the women were envious and said they wished their husbands had kissed them like that. Michael thought it would be a better cruise if he could get the business at hand out of the way and just enjoy the time with Eve.

Back in the room, after dinner, Michael said, "Well, there aren't many things you're not supposed to do while working undercover. Winning awards in front of the entire group of passengers and crew and bringing attention to yourself is probably at the top of the list."

"Well," said Eve looking innocent, "it was your fault for kissing me."

"It was *your* fault for looking adorable," he countered.

"Me? Adorable? Next thing you'll say is I'm irresistible." She started to undo her blouse.

"Again? Well, missy, two can play that game."

Soon, they were standing together, naked. They crawled into bed and made love softly and slowly, enjoying the feel of each other's body and the pleasure of love simmering for hours.

Eighteen

A sliver of sunlight pierced the curtains. The cruise was so smooth it was hard to tell whether they were moving. Eve, ever mindful that they might be moored where outsiders could see into their room, held the curtains closed and peeked out.

"Like yesterday," she said. "There is a park, with couples walking and playing – frisbee for one. I've lost track. Where are we?"

"Today we see Strasbourg – our only stop in France. Maybe we'll have better luck today." He walked to the door. "I'll hit breakfast early and dawdle. When you get ready, we can extend our breakfast stay a little longer – just in case 'they' come in later."

Eve took a little time getting ready, but the breakfasts, like every other meal on the ship, were fabulous, and she didn't want to miss the chance for a great meal. *I'll have to exercise some portion control.* The ghost of her overweight past was always in the shadows.

Michael was at a table in another area of the restaurant from where they'd sat the night before. He was one table over from the table where the congressman had been sitting for dinner, but there was no sign of either of them.

"Well, I would explain," he was saying to an older couple he was sitting with, "but frankly, unless you are actually in insurance, it is pretty dull. Even some in the business think it's dull." He stood when Eve approached. "There you are, dear. I was just talking with Bill and Betty McCullough. Bill is the president of a bank in Kansas City. Betty tries to keep him out of trouble and has her hands full with the house, yard, kids, and everything that goes along with that." Bill and Betty were smiling, then laughing at what Michael had said.

Michael started to kiss Eve, but she allowed only a short 'good morning' kiss. "No need to try to win any more awards, dear," she said with a smile.

Eve had an omelet, juice, and toast. When offered champagne, she couldn't think of a decent reason to refuse. Michael took a glass too, and before drinking, touched her glass with his. The McCulloughs excused themselves saying they had to get some things ready to go for the city tour.

"Well," said Michael, "I guess breakfast was a bust."

"Speak for yourself, this is delicious."

"You know what I mean. I need to get close to those two, if only for a short time. And, of course, get a few pictures – if possible. Our philandering friend may be camera shy."

"So, what do you suggest?" She thought about using the word propose, but she didn't want to scare Michael. Besides, it was WAY too early to even start thinking that way. Still . . .

"I'll try to get some from a distance, when they don't know they are being photographed. If the photos turn up, I don't want anyone to be able to trace them back to us. I want it to be more of a 'how did they get these' moment."

"Well," she said, "we'd better get going, too, or we'll miss the tour."

They grabbed their things from their stateroom and headed for the boarding/disembarking area. They picked up their re-boarding passes and headed off the ship, up the ramp, and to the road where the buses were parked. There were only a few seats left, and they had to walk to the back of the bus. On the way, they passed the congressman and his lady.

The bus trip was short, but before they could connect with the two, they were directed to a separate group. Michael told the cruise director that a friend was in the group containing the congressman, and got them switched.

Strasbourg turned out to be a beautiful Medieval city. The tour wound across and back over the Ill River. Sandstone churches, cathedrals, and black on white timber framed buildings transported Eve and Michael back in time.

"This is absolutely beautiful," said Eve, a sense of wonder evident in her voice.

"Yes.Yes, it is," said Michael. "You couldn't get a bad picture here if you tried. If it weren't for the tourists, you could really imagine you were back in Medieval times."

"Along with the attendant roving gangs, plagues, and other things bent on taking life away."

"Wow! For a beautiful woman, you sure know how to deliver a buzz kill."

"Sorry. It just crept out. I took a fair amount of history in college. Our professor didn't want us to romanticize earlier times. So, he made sure to emphasize the bad side of things."

"Sounds like he needed to get laid."

"Probably," she said, "although he most likely would have gone on about how easily one could get the pox – syphilis. Never a good conversation to have before – you know."

They were both laughing. "Yes, I know," he said. "And thank you."

"I'm not sure whether I should say 'You're welcome' or 'No, thank YOU,' sir."

They continued to shadow their prey. Michael was able to get a short video on his phone, but a review showed it wasn't good enough for what he needed. Whenever they seemed close, the two would head in another direction, or dart through a door. Following would have been obvious. All too soon, it was time to either split off from the group and spend the day in the city, or board the bus and head back to the ship. Eve secretly hoped they could stay in the city – it was so beautiful. It was not to be. The congressman, somewhat belatedly, headed for the bus. Eve and Michael followed, but the bus boarded by the congressman was full, and they had to take a second.

"Can't seem to catch a break," he said. "I might have to try to force something, but that is always risky. I don't want to get made." Eve looked at him and cocked one eye. "That's not what I mean, and you know it. By the way, I must not be used to the kind of work out we did yesterday. I'm a little sore in places."

"I don't feel sorry for you. I think I may have pulled some muscles."

"Oh, I wasn't looking for sympathy. I was bragging."

She hit his arm playfully.

Nineteen

Back on the boat, they decided to head for some lunch before figuring out how to catch the congressman. They walked into a sparsely filled restaurant. Toward the center, at a table by themselves were the congressman and the girl.

"Smile, sweetie. Let's hope this works."

They walked up to the table and Michael said, "Hi! We haven't had the pleasure. I'm George Franklin, and this is my lovely wife, Evelyn Bellow. It seems like such a shame to sit by ourselves when there are good people to meet."

The congressman was overweight and obviously out of shape. His long salt and pepper hair was slicked straight back, as if trying to cover the diminishing thickness in his scalp. He wore a long-sleeved, light blue button-down shirt and dress slacks. *Looks like he just came from the office*, Eve thought, *and with no sense of fashion*. The young lady was wearing pink mid-thigh shorts and a short-sleeved white blouse. Both fit well – not too tight, and not too loose. A set of white Keds completed the look. *Nice look. Her hair would probably look better in a pony tail, but that would probably make her look like she was twelve years old. Too much makeup, but she's probably trying to look older for – him?*

The congressman appeared skeptical until Eve started to turn on the charm – just a bit. She plopped into the chair next to him, placing her hand ever so lightly on his forearm. "George, my husband," she started, "is an insurance underwriter. But don't worry. I've made him promise not to talk insurance while we are on this trip." She rubbed her hand ever so slightly up and down his arm. Michael noticed because he was looking for it. The girl did not.

"Sure. Sure. I'm Frank Smith, and this is – um, Susan."

"Nice to meet you, Frank," said Michael. *Frank Smith. Really? I guess creativity isn't his strong suit.*

"I, of course," continued Eve as she removed her hand from Frank's arm, "have a small-ish but thriving fashion design business in San Francisco – Evening Fashions by Evelyn B. It's small, most folks haven't heard of it. But they do seem to ask why George and I have different last names. I had the business before I met George, and people just expect me to keep my same name. I asked, but George just wouldn't change his last name to Bellow." Frank, Michael and Eve were laughing.

Susan looked at Eve with big eyes. "You're a fashion designer?! I've never met a real-life fashion designer. That's so – so cool. Could I talk to you about your business? I'd love to be a fashion designer when . . ."

"I'm sure Mrs. Bellow is too busy for that," Frank said, hurriedly, cutting her off.

Probably didn't want her to say 'when I grow up.' Bastard. "No, really. I'm always interested in talking fashion. And, unlike insurance, some people like to talk about fashion," finished Eve, smiling and winking at Michael.

"Frank," started Michael, "I've got a couple of truly great cigars. Why don't we get a whiskey and head out to the outdoor lounge? The ladies will just bore us – not to mention pester us until they get their way." Frank seemed skeptical. "What do you drink, Frank? Bourbon?"

"Well," Frank started to say slowly, "actually, yes. Bourbon."

Probably afraid the girl will say more than he wants her to, thought Eve.

"I do believe I saw a bottle of Pappy Van Winkle up there," said Michael. "You in? My treat."

At the mention of a bourbon that goes for more than three thousand dollars a bottle, it seemed that any negative consequences must have vanished from Frank's mind, especially if someone else was paying.

"Why sure. Always time for a sip and a smoke," Frank said, smiling.

Michael bought the whiskey and pulled out the cigars from a case he had in his pocket. They headed forward to the outdoor lounge.

When they had gone, Eve turned to the girl. "So, Susan, what interests you about fashion, anything in particular?"

"Everything! Just EVERYTHING! I mean, how do you dream up all those beautiful clothes? I'd love to be able to do that, but I don't think I'm creative enough or smart enough, you know."

"Well, you have to learn. And there are lots of things to learn. Would you like to see some of the things in our catalog?"

"Would I?! I can't believe I'm sitting here with you. This is so – so cool."

Eve was glad she'd dropped one of the made-up catalogs into her bag – just in case.

When she opened it, Susan said, "You did all these?! Oh, my gosh! These are beautiful! Beautiful!"

Eve's heart sank. *This sweet, innocent girl is going to be the center of a firestorm in a short time. Her life might be ruined, and we are going to do it to her. But, if we don't do it now, she won't be the last.* The thought didn't make her feel any less a sense of betrayal.

Susan's eyes were huge. She looked at the fashions, then at Eve, then back at the fashions. "These are – they're just so beautiful."

"How about this," Eve heard herself say. "Do you like this one? How about this one?"

"Oh, yes. Yes."

"You seem so sweet, and I know you are interested. How about I send these two to you – on me."

"Really? You could do that?"

"Trust me. I know the owner of the store." Eve started to laugh, then Susan laughed. "Just between us girls, though.

Our secret. Promise?"

"I don't have anything to write my address on," said Susan. "And, yes, for sure, our secret." Susan looked through her clutch purse. "Do you have a camera? I have my driver's license. You could take a picture of that. But don't tell him," she said, looking in the direction of the two men on the bow of the ship. Susan pulled out her license. "It's still kind of new. My real name is Missy. It's short for Melissa. He wants me to tell everyone my name is Susan because it sounds older than Missy."

Eve's vision began to lose focus. She could barely contain herself. *This girl is barely eighteen.* She felt sadness and pity for this girl and for what she was about to be put through, anger and hatred for the animal who had brought her here.

Missy was talking. "His name isn't really Frank, either. He says people wouldn't understand. We have to pretend to be Susan and Frank."

Eve snapped a picture of the girl's license and checked to make sure it was clear. "Well, I don't want to get you in trouble, so we should keep each other's secrets. Okay?"

"Okay, for sure. And thank you. Are you really going to send me those two dresses? They're beautiful."

"Of course, I will. What size are you – about a four?"

"How did you know? Oh, that's right you do this for a living."

Eve picked up her phone and dialed a number. On the other end, Meg picked up. "What's up?"

"Yes. Hi. This is Evelyn. That's right. How's the weather in San Francisco?" Eve was hoping that Missy wouldn't figure out that it was about four in the morning in San Francisco, the pretend home of her pretend business. "Listen, I met this lovely young lady on the cruise. I'd like to have two dresses sent out to her as soon as you can."

"What is this about?" asked Meg, not quite getting it.

"Yes, two dresses. Size four. Item numbers," Eve read off the item numbers. She'd picked two dresses she knew they had on hand. "That's right," Eve was saying. Meg was quiet. "They need to go to, make sure you get the address right."

"You really want the dresses sent?" asked Meg finally.

"Yes. Bill them to my account. Check with John Digby to be sure everything is as it should be." She knew that at the mention of John Digby, Meg would understand. This had to do with the 'job' Michael had taken her on. "The name," she continued quietly, "of the young lady is Missy Johnson." She then read off the address. "Second day should be good enough. They will be there when she gets home."

Eve hung up and turned to Missy. "There. They should be waiting for you when you get home. And remember, our secret."

"Oh, thank you. Thank you. Thank you," said Missy, wrapping her arms around Eve's neck. Eve felt dirty knowing that two dresses were a very cheap price for what the world would do when Missy's identity came out.

Eve put her bag on the table. Within two minutes, Michael and Frank came in from outside, talking like two chums.

"How are you doing, Sweetheart?" asked Michael.

"Not so well," answered Eve. "I think the morning took more out of me than I realized. I need to lie down for a bit. Be a dear and get me some water." She turned to Frank and said, "Sorry to run off like this. I just need to rest." She put on her best face, but she wanted to rip his off.

"Not at all, my dear. Not at all."

Eve turned to Missy, "It was nice chatting with you, Susan. Maybe we can sit together at dinner." Then, she allowed Michael to escort her out of the restaurant and to the stateroom.

Twenty

"Eighteen, Michael! She's barely eighteen!" Eve was trying to contain herself, but she was having trouble. "This – this animal, this pig!"

Michael was trying to calm her down. "I know. I know. That's why we're here. It has to stop, and we're going to stop it. That's why we're here."

"So, what happens to her when the story breaks? What happens to her? I know what happens to her. She's in the middle of a firestorm, and her life is ruined. No matter what we do." She was crying.

"Okay, look," he said. He tried to put his arms around her, but she put her hand out, keeping him at bay. "He's done this before got a girl – not woman, girl – pregnant. Forced her to get an abortion and paid her off. He won't stop until he's stopped."

"But her life," she started, but didn't finish.

"Yes. I know that they," he said pointing upward, "will do what they can to protect her as much as they can. But the alternative is to do nothing. Her life will be ruined, and so will the next girl's and the one after that."

"Don't you have any feeling for her, though?"

"Yes. But I also feel for the next ones who will be protected. If we could have done this with the first girl, we wouldn't have to be arguing about Missy's future. I try to focus on the job. They're not all fun, but they need to be done."

"Don't you feel . . ."

"Yeah. Rotten. We can't send the picture of her license. First, it would be too easy to leak that information. We'll protect her as best as we can here and hope the boss will do the same."

There was a knock at the door. Eve wiped the tears from her eyes, stood, and walked over. When she opened the door, she was surprised to see Missy standing there.

"I hope I'm not bothering you. You said you weren't feeling well and I wanted to check to see if there was anything I could do. I mean, you were so nice to me. Is this a good time?"

"Of course," said Eve. Turning so Missy couldn't see her face, Eve looked at Michael, opened her eyes as wide as she could, and gave a questioning look. When she turned back to Missy, she said, "Please come in. Mich – George was just going up to do some exercises on the sun deck, weren't you, dear?"

"Um, yes. Actually, Susan, your timing is perfect." Michael grabbed a bottle of water and as he headed out the door, he put his little finger and thumb to the side of his face in a 'call me' gesture.

"So," Eve started as soon as the door closed. "I'm doing okay, just a little more tired than I expected. Did you want to talk?" She offered a bottle of water to Missy, opened one herself, and took a drink.

"Actually, yes. You aren't tired because you're pregnant, are you?" asked Missy.

Eve spit water out her mouth and nose, coughing and choking.

"Oh, gosh! Did I say something wrong?"

Eve recovered sufficiently to say, "No. No, dear. You just caught me off guard. We aren't quite ready to start a family – yet."

"Oh. I just thought that one reason a woman gets tired out more easily than usual . . ." Missy let the thought die out.

"You aren't?"

"Oh, no. Not yet, anyway," said Missy. Eve suddenly wished she had a shot of the whiskey the guys were drinking earlier. This conversation was getting 'too real' too fast.

"I know he's older than I am. People would talk. He has a job that – well, he kind of gets a new contract every two years. That contract needs to be renewed this year, so we have to be secret until after the elec – 'til then. The other reason is he's married. After the – the contract is renewed, he's going to leave his wife and we can be married."

Eve was just staring. No words would come to her.

"We've only had," Missy looked down, "sex a few times. He said since we were going to be married anyway, there wasn't any need for, you know, protection."

Eve couldn't decide whether she was angry, sad, hopeless, or what. She wanted to say, "You little naïve girl," but she knew that would be the worst thing she could do.

"I didn't tell him," Missy continued, "but I started taking birth control pills. I mean, once we're actually married . . ." Again, the thought was left unfinished.

Eve breathed a sigh of partial relief. She felt sadness and pity for a girl – yes, girl – who had been lied to and taken advantage of. Michael was right. This animal had to be stopped. In her mind, all she could picture was 'Frank' bound and gagged while she loaded a revolver – a look of horror on his face.

"I'm really glad you trusted me and came to talk with me," said Eve, her mind racing to try to figure out what to say next. "And, I think you're smart," at the word smart, Missy perked up, "to take the birth control. I mean, if his, um contract, isn't renewed – well, sometimes things change. A girl has to protect herself." Eve wasn't even sure if she was making sense. "But you can come to me anytime you want to talk. And maybe we can sit together at dinner."

"Thank you so much, Mrs. Bellow."

"Please, call me Evelyn," Eve said, knowing she was keeping the deception going, and one thing Missy didn't need was more deception. "And, thank you for trusting me." That sick feeling again when she knew that Missy's 'trust' would only result in betrayal.

She walked Missy to the door and let her out. When the door closed, Eve collapsed against it, tears forming in her eyes. She saw her phone on the nightstand and thought, *Now, I need somebody to talk to*. She picked up the phone and punched in the numbers.

Twenty-one

Meg answered Eve's call on the third ring – a seemingly infinite amount of time for Eve on the other end.

"Hello? Eve?"

You're not going to believe this! I'm not sure I quite believe it myself."

"What's going on?" asked Meg while Eve seemingly babbled on.

Eve couldn't quite get it out. She knew Meg must be frustrated but she also knew she wouldn't hang up on her best friend who had apparently called because she needed a lifeline. Finally, she calmed.

"Oh, my God," was how she started. "I don't know where to start. I thought – I thought I'd see what this was like. What it would be to see what 'Digby' did for a living. I thought we'd do something for justice, have a good time. It would all be fun and games. But this congressman is a pig. Just shooting him wouldn't be good enough. At the least, he should be castrated with a dull knife – maybe a hammer."

Meg winced, but knew Eve had her reasons.

Over the next twenty minutes, Eve went through what they had found out. Meg was surprised at the language Eve used when she talked about 'Frank.' While they talked, Meg looked him up on the internet. There he was – Southern gentleman, posing with his wife and grown children, all smiles, family values. Meg agreed. He was a real bastard. When Eve got to the part about him not wanting to use contraceptives, she was ready to buy the hammer for Eve to use for his castration.

Then, Eve started to tell her about this beautiful girl – naive girl really for believing the pack of lies she been fed – and how her life was going to be destroyed when all this came out.

"I don't know how, how I'm going to deal with all of this, much less her," she confided. "I feel like such a rat."

Eve heard Meg call to her husband, John, who had been known as 'Digby' before Michael.

"Hi, Eve. How are you doing?"

"I feel rotten."

"Because of the girl, or because you can't just shoot the congressman?"

"Shooting is too good for him, but I won't go through what I'd like to do."

"Okay," Eve heard him start. "The girl then. Yeah, you feel rotten. Even if she's never identified, this is still going to be very traumatic for her. But the guy was never going to leave his wife and marry her. The wife has the family money, and his family values support would go right out the window. No. And, he'll drop the girl as soon as he's tired of her. So, while you may not feel any better with me saying this, the trauma of finding out that he's going to dump her and the trauma of 'losing' him when this explodes – those are kind of a wash. Not easy to hear, but it's the truth.

"But when it comes out that . . ."

"It's never a sure thing that she won't become known, but trust me, the boss does his best to keep the innocents protected. Her identity won't be revealed unless there is no other way – and then, it will be revealed to a select few."

I've got a picture – on my phone - of her driver's license.

"Don't send that to anyone," said John. "Michael can take a picture of the picture on your phone. Then, you can delete yours. If you send it – anywhere – there is a record. We don't want that."

Eve was starting to feel a little better. "Michael was talking about getting some pictures. I'm worried that she could be identified from those."

"Don't worry. In a case like this, even with great pictures, when released, the young lady will be 'fuzzed' enough so she can't be identified. The gentleman will be very clear."

"Thank you. I feel a little better now. Now that you've explained those things."

"I'm sure Michael would have, too, but you have to remember, he's in the middle of this. He's trying to do the job and do it right. And, protect you. By the way, you are doing fantastic. Just remember, you're keeping another girl from going through this later. By the way, the dresses were packed up. I sent them off to a friend in San Francisco – overnight. When your young lady receives them, they will look like they came from SF."

"Thank you, John. Can I have Meg back?"

"Feeling better?" asked Meg.

"Yeah, some. I still have the feeling, you know, that I'm lying to this girl who needs my help desperately. The truth is, I AM lying to her. And I feel rotten betraying her."

"I know, but remember what John said. At some time in the future, she's not going to have this," Meg let the thought die, not sure what word would adequately describe Frank. "It can be because he outright dumps her, and I'm sure he's not going to be too kind. By the way, if it makes you feel any better, when his wife, family, and constituents find out, any one of them might just shoot him. At the very least, without his wife's money he'll probably be working the midnight shift at some fast food place."

"Unless he slithers off somehow."

"I don't think that's going to happen, sweetie. So, any other news, not that you could top that."

"No. Not really. Well, Michael and I had sex."

"WHAT!?"

"Michael and I had sex."

"Sweetie, I know you were feeling bad about the girl

and all, but this should have been the lead. Really. Get a glass of wine. Make yourself comfy, and tell your aunt Meg all about it. And I mean ALL about it."

Over the next twenty minutes, Eve related what had happened the day – and night – before; the kisses at breakfast, the sunscreen on the bus, everything leading up to when they were back on the boat.

"When he started to rub the sunscreen in, I just about melted. Somehow, he knew what it was doing to me . . ."

"He used to work as a masseuse."

"He what? How do you know that?"

"John told me," said Meg. "He went to school. A story he was doing. Apparently, he's pretty good."

"Pretty good?! All he did was my upper back and shoulders and I almost had an orgasm."

"And you did what?"

"I couldn't let him get away with that, so I put my hand on his thigh and sort of gave it a rub if I saw something interesting out the window that I wanted to point out."

"And?"

"It was a very interesting city." By now both women were laughing. "So, we were all hot and sweaty when we got back to the boat," continued Eve. "I said I should shower, but apparently that wasn't on the dance card. He told me that if I wanted him to stop, I should tell him then, because in another few seconds, it would be too late."

"So, did you tell him to stop?" asked Meg.

"Are you kidding? In about two seconds, we were ripping, and I mean ripping, each other's clothes off. We were like two minks. I'm not sure some of the sounds I was making were even human. And then, all of a sudden, time stopped just before the universe exploded."

"You know, I'd love to make a Big Bang joke here, but it just won't come to me."

"Ha. Ha. After we recovered and the ability to think and speak returned, we were hotter and sweatier. I showered, then he showered. When he came out into the room, I was in a robe, with my hair in a towel. After he looked at me for a few seconds, his little friend started poking his head out of his robe. So, we were off to the races once again. Meg? You there?"

"Um, yeah. I was just thinking about something I need to take care of."

"Well, I'm afraid Michael has a few claw marks in his back. I've got some sore muscles – no comments, please, and at least one bruise – and no, I don't mean THERE. Well, I could mean there. I mean . . ." Eve paused. "Never mind."

Eve told her about their award and spending the night together naked. "But now, now I don't know what I'm feeling. Yesterday was so great, but we've just met, and things are moving really, really fast. I think too fast. I'm not sure what or how I should be feeling."

"Well, of course you don't," said Meg. "First of all, like you said, you just met, and frankly my dear, you're not used to being swept off your feet. Love is scary. You'll have all kinds of feelings, and, unfortunately, doubts. You don't have to expect everything will fall into place immediately. Take your time. You just need to sort everything out – it takes time. But even in the end, it won't be logical or a sure thing. But you'll know what's right."

"Thanks – I think."

"And, don't forget, this adventure you're on – it's stressful, and probably more than you're used to dealing with."

"Okay. Thank you – and John, again. I'd better call Michael. He'll be wondering what took so long." As Eve hung up the phone, she heard Meg say, "John, could you come here? I need your help." What she didn't know was that after Eve's accounting of the night before, Meg was unbuttoning the second and third buttons on her blouse.

Eve dialed in Michael's number. After finishing his workout, he was having a glass of cranberry juice in the lounge.

Twenty-two

Michael entered the stateroom carrying a bottle of cranberry juice and a bottle ginger ale. "That took a while. She must have really unburdened herself."

"Well, she did have some things she told me. She thinks the congressman is going to marry her. Actually, I think she may suspect he won't marry her. She's afraid. And, get this, the congressman told her that because they're going to be married anyway, she doesn't have to worry about him not using prevention. At least she's had the good sense to start taking birth control pills without him knowing it."

"Jesus! This guy really is a piece of work."

"He's a piece of something all right. So, what do we do next?"

"People are pretty much creatures of habit. They are expecting us to maybe sit at dinner with them. Most likely, they will sit at the same table they've been sitting at. I'd like to get there first, pick our two seats and save two for them. I've got a couple of small cameras. I'll use one at the table to get some pictures of them together. I can plant one in the hallway and see if I can get them entering their room together."

"Won't they see you taking pictures of them?"

"I don't think so. Wait a minute." He went into the bathroom and returned in a couple of minutes.

"You okay?" asked Eve.

"Uh, yeah, sure. As I was beginning to say, I'll get some pictures of them at dinner, and I'll hide another camera in the passageway to get pictures of them going into their room."

"I can't believe you're going to get pictures of them without them seeing you."

"Why not?"

"Because they're going to see the camera. They're going to see you taking their picture."

"So, I guess you saw me take six pictures of you while we were sitting here?"

"You what!?"

"When I went to the bathroom, I put on a camera, I think you'll agree it is small enough and hidden well enough that it is difficult to see. And, I can shoot pictures without holding the camera up and saying 'cheese,' okay?"

"Oh, my . . . Wait a minute. Have you taken any *other* pictures of me without my knowing it?" Eve nodded toward the bed.

"No. Never. I wouldn't. Well, unless you want me to. Eight by ten glossy – maybe a few wallet sized?" They both laughed.

"Okay, so they are small enough to be hidden. Aren't you afraid that once the pictures come out, they'll know who took them?"

"No, I'll get them in a way that it could have been someone walking by the table. And, this will be the only night we will be sitting with them. We'll find someone equally as fascinating tomorrow night. Well, unless your new-found friend presses you into sitting by her for the next few nights. You've befriended her, and she may want you around so she can feel safe."

"Or, she can want me not around so that he won't suspect anything."

"You know," said Michael, "I've never understood women."

"You know," countered Eve, "neither have I."

"Okay," he laughed, "one other thing. I'm going to have you go down to dinner first and grab the seats at the table – and reserve two spots for them. As soon as they enter the restaurant, flag them down, and apologize for me not being there. Then, send me a text message they have arrived. I'll be down in a couple of minutes."

"What are you going to do?"

"I'll let you know later. Don't worry."

"Right. I do want you to know that one of the reasons it took so long this afternoon was that I called Meg after Missy left. I needed to talk to her. I feel kind of rotten lying to this little girl and knowing that, in part because she trusts me, her life is going to be pure hell in a short time."

He pulled her to the bed, where they both sat. "Look, I know this isn't any fun. I don't like doing it either. When the story comes out, everyone will do their best to protect her while exposing him. No one hundred percent guarantees, but we'll try our best."

"Oh, I almost forgot, the picture of her license. While I was on the phone with Meg, John mentioned I shouldn't send it to you. There'd be a record."

"Lemme see," he said. "Jesus! Eighteen! I hope his constituents string him up – run him out of town on a rail at the very least. Well, if he's alive after his wife gets ahold of him." Michael got his cell phone and took a photograph of the picture on Eve's phone. "There, I got it. Now erase it from your phone."

She did as he'd asked. "So, could they really trace it?"

"Yes, it's possible. This way, now I'm the only one with it. You're clean. I don't want you involved – well, I don't want you to have any provable involvement. If they bust me, look for Digby to be doing his column out of a small village in the Himalayas."

She looked at him. "You're kidding, right?"

"Depending what friends this guy has, if I'm burned, the boss will move me to someplace safe, aka, totally out of the way. I may not even be doing writing. I may be flipping flap jacks – or whatever they eat there – Yak burgers? Anyway, we should probably get ready for the daily briefing, then dinner."

Eve was mildly concerned about what might happen to him. In part because she wasn't quite sure yet, but he *might* be the one. And, she thought, she wouldn't want to end up being a waitress in some dive in the Himalayas carrying yak burgers to the customers.

"Oh, before we change . . ." she started.

"Yes?"

"Put the cameras in a drawer – all of them," she said with a smile.

He removed a camera. The lens was apparently taking the place of a button on his shirt. He placed that camera and two more – small enough that they amazed her – into a drawer and closed it. "Happy, Dear?" he asked smiling.

"Well, satisfied that my privacy won't be breached, anyway," she replied with a smile.

Twenty-three

She decided on a multi-colored printed casual dress that came to mid-thigh and a pair of natural sandals. Michael wore charcoal slacks and a blue short-sleeved guayabera with dark blue buttons. Just before dinner, Eve headed to the door to go to the dining room.

"Remember, when they enter the restaurant, send me a text message," he reminded her.

"Got it. It's a simple thing to do. I do it every day. So, why do I feel nervous about it now? And, what will you be doing?"

"As far as you're concerned, I'm just going to rest in the stateroom for a few minutes until our friends show up for dinner."

"Uh huh. Why am I having trouble believing that?"

"Probably your suspicious nature, dear," he said with a smile.

"So, we're not going to go to prison?"

"Well, not you, anyway," he said and kissed her on the cheek.

Eve entered the restaurant, walked up the right side, and stopped at the table where Frank and Missy had dined every meal so far. She hoped they would follow a familiar pattern and head there once again. She picked a seat facing the restaurant entrance and crossed the utensils on two settings, indicating those places were already taken.

A waiter came over and gave her a menu for the evening. He asked if she wanted anything to drink.

"Champagne, perhaps, Madame?"

"Yes. Thank you. That would be lovely. My husband should be right down. Could you bring one for him, as well?"

"Certainly. Also, we have a selection for this evening. May I suggest the Caesar salad and the beef tenderloin. Both are excellent."

"Thank you. I think I'll wait for Mich – my husband before I order, if that's okay." Eve silently chided herself for almost using Michael's real name.

"Certainly. Thank you, Madame."

The waiter delivered the champagne. She wanted to shoot the first glass and get a second, maybe a third, but she decided she should try to act 'lady-like' and sip the champagne. *Why am I so nervous? All I have to do is send a text. I don't even know what Michael is going to do. Maybe that's why I'm so nervous.*

She finished her champagne and was eyeing Michael's. She decided to place her empty glass at his setting and take his. *He can always get another*, she mused. *I don't know what he has planned, but this waiting is driving me crazy.* She swapped glasses and as the waiter walked by asked that

'Michael's' glass be refilled. The waiter smiled and said, "Yes, Madame. It is an odd phenomenon, but those glasses always seem to leak."

Just as the waiter was bringing a fresh glass to Michael's place, Frank entered the restaurant. Eve started to panic. *What if Missy isn't going to have dinner this evening? Should I text Michael? Should I not text Michael? Why didn't we talk about this?* She slowed down. *He wants them to be here, so he must want them out of their room – god, what is he planning? I won't text unless both of them are here. I'm more nervous now than before. How does he do this?*

She stood and waved. "Frank!"

Frank turned, looked over, and saw her standing at the table where he and Missy usually ate. He looked a little wary, but Eve was by herself. She could see that he was eyeing the dress she was wearing – it showed off her legs, a bit higher than mid-thigh when she waved, and the casual dress she wore gave a glimpse down her décolletage. *There wasn't any way he was going to pass this up*, she thought.

"Well, hello, Evelyn," he started. "Um, your husband . . .?"

"He's in the room. Taking care of a few last-minute things. Susan?"

"She'll be here in a minute."

"Well, I thought we could sit together this evening. You seem like such lovely people. I thought I'd save you a couple of seats." She smiled at him and flipped her hair. Then, she bent as if to indicate the seats she'd saved. In doing so, she intentionally exposed a bit more cleavage. The smile she'd forced became real when she saw that Frank was hooked. *Got him*! she thought.

"Well, certainly. I might have a glass of champagne, as well."

About that time, Missy entered the restaurant. She was wearing a sundress and white sandals. Her hair was down, and she was again wearing more makeup than she should have been wearing.

Makeup's a little thick, thought Eve, *but not badly done. Makes her look older – maybe almost legal –* she looked at Frank and forced a smile – *pig. Without makeup and hair in a pony tail, you'd think she was twelve.*

"Well, where is that man?" said Eve out loud. I'd better check on him. She got out her phone and with shaking hands, managed to send a text. She double checked the phone number to make sure she'd at least gotten that right.

Down in the stateroom, Michael's mobile phone buzzed. He got up from the bed and went to the sliding door, opened it and stepped onto their small balcony. He took a deep breath and checked to make sure the small camera was in his shirt pocket. In a quick move, he slid around the partition separating their balcony from the one next door. He knew from knocking on their door earlier that the stateroom would be empty. His biggest concern was that for a second, he would be hanging off the side of the ship and visible to anyone who might be looking down from above or from security cameras mounted on the sides of the ship to ensure that guest staterooms weren't burgled – essentially what he was doing now.

He walked to the next partition and knew that the target stateroom was above and over. He said a quick prayer and even while doing so thought, *I'm sure God doesn't protect those who go surreptitiously trying to get pictures, even if the pictures are of miscreants.* He checked to be sure no one was looking, then, in a quick move, he climbed diagonally up and onto the balcony outside Frank and Susan's stateroom. He was going to plant a camera on the railing, but he took a chance and pulled on the sliding glass door. It opened. He couldn't believe his luck. He quickly entered the room, looked around, and planted the micro camera under an upper cabinet. It had a clear view of the bed. He shook his head and thought, *the things I do for this job.* He walked to the door, opened it carefully and found no one in the passageway. He left the stateroom and headed to the restaurant.

Twenty-four

Eve was sitting in the restaurant at a table with Frank and Missy, trying to make small talk while wondering where Michael was and what he was doing. Then she thought, *maybe it's better if I don't know what he's doing. Plausible deniability.* She managed to get Missy between herself and Frank, not a particularly easy thing to do with Frank ogling her cleavage and pushing Missy out of the way.

Eve had said, "Susan, why don't you sit next to me. We can talk about girl things. Those always bore the boys." Then, she had ushered Missy to the chair, smiling at Frank all the while thinking, *pig. You've duped this innocent girl into coming with you, now all you want to do is stare at my breasts.*

Eve gave a sigh of relief when she saw Michael enter the restaurant, smoothing the front of his shirt with his hands. He looked toward the table and when he saw Eve, he smiled broadly. She thought to herself, *he really does look good. I wonder if those are tailored. They fit great, and he's got some great places they have to fit around.* In the few seconds it took for him to cross to the table, she took in his broad shoulders, muscular arms and forearms. He had strong hands, and she thought about how strong they were and at the same time how soft they felt when he was applying sunscreen to her back.

His shirt draped down his shoulders and over his pects. It hung straight down, not touching his stomach. She also noted that he moved with a certain grace, like a cat, smooth, economical, but with a hint of power and strength. Her mind started to drift back to the day they had come back from the tour of Strasbourg and, well, fell into bed like two minks.

"Hi folks. Sorry I'm late. Frank, nice to see you – and Susan, as well. I was – oh, thank you dear," he said spotting the champagne.

Eve put her hand on the back of his chair. Michael took her hand and kissed it, then kissed her on the cheek. Still standing, he picked up the flute toasted his wife, and said, "Good times."

Eve knew that one of the buttons on the shirt had to be the camera lens, but she couldn't see it. *How would he do this? Would he put it up higher so he could get pictures during dinner, or lower so that the lens would be covered when he sat – so nobody would see? I can't believe I'm thinking about this. But he seems to be standing for longer than I would have thought.*

"I'm so glad we could join you for dinner, at least for tonight. Maybe it's the extrovert in me – you can't not like meeting people in my business – I just enjoy meeting new people." Michael sat next to Eve. He had the flute in his right hand. He placed his left hand under the table cloth and on Eve's bare thigh, below the hem of her dress, which had exposed more thigh when she was seated.

Eve felt her stomach do a little flip and her heart do a little flutter. Somewhere inside, a tingling warmth.

Michael sipped the champagne and said, "This is really

good. Have you tasted it?"

"Um, yes. Your first glass was defective. I had to get rid of it. Mine too."

Michael laughed. "I guess I have some catching up to do."

"So, Frank," Michael said, looking over at him, "tell me about this auto sales business you have. I'm interested in learning more."

Seeing as how it's your wife's business, thought Eve. Michael had briefed her about 'Frank' and his family. Frank's wife held the keys – the financial keys, that is – to Frank's kingdom. Without her, he was basically financially broke. That was one of the reasons Frank would never leave his wife, no matter how much he promised these girls.

Frank started to talk. Eve noted that he was wearing a short-sleeved shirt, doughy white arms extending from the sleeves. He was overweight, probably from the cushy lifestyle he enjoyed, and appeared to be terribly out of shape. Maybe it was because of what he was doing – AND running on a family values, wholesome image platform. *How could anyone be interested in him?* - Eve tried to keep from shuddering visibly, but she couldn't.

Michael broke off the conversation, looked at her and said, "You okay, dear?"

"Just a quick chill. I'm fine."

"Good," he said. Then, he rubbed her thigh with his

hand as he looked into her eyes.

She felt a tingle run through her entire body. Not to be outdone, she put her hand on his thigh – a bit higher than his was on hers, and leaned in to kiss him on the cheek. As she did so, she slid her hand much higher on his thigh. She kissed his cheek and then winked at him.

Michael started to talk, had to clear his throat, then returned to the conversation with Frank about 'his' auto sales business.

Eve looked at Missy. She seemed somewhat lost, both because of the conversation between Michael and Frank and because – *well, maybe it's just me* – of everything else that was going on. "So, what would you like to talk about, Susan?"

Missy brightened up and said, "Could we talk about how you started out in your business – you know, so I could get an idea about how I could start mine someday?"

"Sure, I'd be happy to." Eve told her about meeting someone in college when she was studying fashion design, telling Missy that the woman she'd met was a business person. She left out the details about the school and about who her partner really was. She talked about wanting to do something other than the corporate route, and the two of them started a small business while they were still in college. Then how they grew the business, getting a lucky break or two along the way. Again, she left out any details that might have indicated who she really was.

"Wow! So, you just started? Weren't you scared?"

asked a wide-eyed Missy.

"Scared? No. I guess we figured we were just giving it a shot and didn't really have anything to lose. We just did it."

"That's amazing! Can we," she lowered her voice, "can we keep in touch?"

Missy said this while Frank and Michael were in conversation. Eve was sure that Frank wouldn't like to hear about Missy keeping in touch with anyone. "Sure," she said. "We'll talk later." In the meantime, Eve was trying to think about how they would keep in touch if the Evelyn that Missy thought she knew was just a phantom.

Dinner was pleasant enough. The table was large enough for eight, and two other couples joined the group. Eve was happy about that because it diverted some attention away from dealing with Frank – and Missy, although Missy seemed a bit clingy.

After dinner, Frank said it was time to head to the stateroom. Eve shuddered again, thinking about what might await Missy. Eve and Michael stayed went downstairs and into the lounge.

"Another glass of champagne, dear?" he asked. "How are you doing? After all those defective glasses, should I be concerned?" He was smiling.

"I'm fine," she answered. "It shouldn't be the defective champagne glasses that concerns you. You should be thinking about what playing with my leg under the table will end up creating. Besides, I was nervous wondering what you were doing and then Frank showed up by himself. The way he was looking at me, I felt like I needed a shower. What were you doing, by the way?"

He explained how he'd crawled along the outside to the ship to plant the camera, then found the sliding glass door open, and used that instead of his original plan.

"You crawled along the outside of the ship! You could have – you might have – now, I'm REALLY glad I didn't know. AND, a cat burglar, to boot. I may need more of this stuff."

"More of a second story man, actually, but it wasn't really that hard. Easy climbs. And, I didn't have to go back the same way. That would have been the hard part."

"And if you had fallen off?"

"You may or may not have heard a loud splash and spent the night alone with Frank and Missy."

"Oh, God! Okay. One more thing. If you put a camera in their stateroom, how are you going to get it back?"

"Not sure, yet. I need to work that out."

The piano started playing. "Would you care to dance, dear?" he asked.

"So, when we're arrested, what happens?" she asked as they made their way to the dance floor.

"I'll make a full confession and swear that you knew nothing about it. You were duped. Will you come see me on visitor's days?"

"Christmas and Easter."

She chuckled at his feigned hurt look. The song playing was slow, and he took her in his arms and pulled her against him. She felt a soft, sensual jolt go through her body. He kissed her ear and she felt a warmth growing within her. He pulled her closer and she felt a now familiar enlargement.

Twenty-five

After half a dozen dances, they were back in the stateroom. Michael had tipped the pianist in order to keep the slow dances coming. The pianist didn't mind. The lounge was fairly empty, and the people there weren't interested in any fast songs. They'd spent their time dancing rubbing their bodies together. By the third dance, Eve's head was resting on Michael's chest. Both were lost in a world of sensual joy.

"I need to check a couple of things," he said, "then I need to make a call."

"Oh no you don't," she challenged. "You've been playing with matches all night long. Now, it's time to put out the fire." She pulled him out of his chair and to her. Her arms were around his back – waist high. She looked into his eyes and kissed him softly. Then, more forcefully. Their mouths met. Their lips parted and their tongues met and caressed each other. She was breathing harder. So was he.

"What the hell," he said. "Work can wait."

He lifted her in his arms and carried her to the bed. He set her down, then she pulled him down on top of her. She rolled over until she was on top of him and started undoing his shirt.

More than an hour later, they both lay panting. Clothes were strewn all over the bed and floor. "I don't know about you," he said, "but I'm not sure the fire is out. But your fireman, however, is just about done."

"So, just twice tonight?" she giggled.

"Unless you want me carried out on a stretcher." He got up and stepped toward the drawers at the far end of the bed. She was looking at his body. Everything was muscled, sculpted. If he'd been in marble, he'd have been the perfect statue. He was, but he was human. Warm, tender when he wanted to be, and an incredible lover – giving more than he took.

"Are you staring at me?" he asked.

"Um, looking. Not staring. Why?"

"Because I was – let's say looking at you in the mirror."

"Why Mr. Thomas! What should a lady do?" She pulled the sheet up to cover her breasts and diverted her eyes in a faux demure way. Then, she directed her gaze at his midsection and raised both eyebrows.

He was growing again. "I'm not sure about three," he said unconvincingly.

"Well, your little friend seems up for the challenge," she giggled.

"Yes, but he doesn't have any brains."

"Here, let Eve help." She dropped the sheet and pulled him to her, carefully, using the 'handle' that seemed to respond vigorously to her touch.

"I just want you to know, I haven't had sex this many times in the last three years."

"You know what they say – practice makes perfect."

His voice was raspy and his breath was deep, fast, and irregular. "That saying – is – actually – perfect prac – practice – makes – per – perfect."

"Well, then, you'll just have to let Eve show you what perfect practice is."

Twenty-five minutes later, Michael was on his back, panting like he'd just run a marathon. In a sense, he had. "You're going to kill me, you know."

"No. You just need to get into sex shape. I mean, you're in great shape for a lot of things, you're just out of shape for sex. By the way, thanks for hanging in there and taking care of me. I feel all warm and cuddly now." She rolled against him and he wrapped himself around her.

An hour later, they opened their eyes after dozing. Eve said she needed to shower. Silently, Michael said 'thank you.' He wasn't sure a fourth time was in the cards. And, Little Michael was looking a little worse for wear.

She headed for the shower. He downloaded the pictures he had taken at dinner. Some were worthless. A couple good. Two were great. Frank had leaned almost across Missy to peer down Eve's cleavage when Eve had leaned forward. The effect was of Frank nestling with Missy. In the second, Frank had his arm around her. Michael looked at the feed from the stateroom. Photos were snapped and sent every ten seconds. The first couple of hours were during dinner, so he deleted those. There wasn't much for the first twenty minutes or so when Frank and Missy were in the stateroom. Then, there were some that were very worthwhile. The best showed Susan on the bed in a baby doll nighty. Frank was in his underwear, talking to her. Another had Missy standing and looking out the glass door with her arms crossed. Frank was, apparently pleading.

"One more place to look," he said as he left the stateroom and headed up to the level where Frank had his love nest. Michael searched the floor, as if looking for something he'd dropped. Bending down to pick the imaginary item up, he put it into his pocket and stumbled. Catching himself on the passageway wall, he deftly removed a small camera he had placed next to the ship's security camera. It had been hidden in the shadow to catch the comings and goings from the stateroom. Back in his room, he downloaded a picture of Frank and Missy entering the stateroom together. *Thank you*, he thought, *for turning so both your faces would be plainly visible.*

Eve came out of the shower in a robe. Her hair was wrapped in a towel. "Get anything?" she asked.

"Oh yes. I think we have all we need." Michael picked up his phone and punched in some numbers. "Hi. Thought I'd call and let you know our plans. I know it's a little late." Michael cocked one eye and looked at Eve. "I was, um, tied up." Eve took the tie off the robe and started wrapping it around her hands. Michael gave her a wary look and returned to the phone. "Yes. Heidelberg tomorrow. I can't wait to see the castle. They've got a wall of all kinds of statues. Lot of history. Okay."

"What was all that about?"

"Just checking in. They like me to do that, from time to time."

"Uh huh. Tied up? Is that a request?"

"At the end of this cruise, they're going to find me here – dead in bed – all my vital juices drained."

"Well, look at it this way," she replied, "at least the undertaker won't be able to get the smile off your face."

Twenty-six

With the morning sun, they discovered the ship had tied up in Mannheim. Breakfast was served, and as usual, it was fabulous. Eve mused about all the calories she was taking in and how it was going to affect her ability to get into her clothes. Michael reminded her that it had only been a few days and she shouldn't worry. "Besides, with all the exercise we're getting, you may actually end up losing weight." But the ghost of past weight issues was there, haunting her.

The schedule called for a tour of Heidelberg. As was the standard procedure, after breakfast, bus assignments were made for the trip to Heidelberg castle. Eve and Michael were assigned to a different bus than Frank and Missy. Michael confided that it was acceptable because he already had everything he needed. Still, Eve waved at Missy as they headed to the area where the buses were parked.

The bus ride up to the castle involved some narrow roads with tight turns. More than once, Eve closed her eyes as the bus they were on squeezed through a narrow uphill intersection. Aside from the mildly terrifying ride, the scenery was magnificent. As the roads ascended the hill to the castle, beautiful views of the Neckar Valley and Heidelberg itself were visible through the wooded hillside.

"They say Mark Twain fell in love with Heidelberg. I can see why. It's just beautiful," she marveled.

"Yes, it is. Wait until you see the castle."

When the buses stopped, they had a short uphill walk to the castle. Eve was wearing pale blue slacks, a white sleeveless top, and blue light walking shoes. Michael was wearing a white short-sleeved shirt with dark blue slacks.

"Heidelberg castle is a Renaissance structure dating from the thirteenth century," began their guide. "It was expanded over the centuries and also partially destroyed by fires, lighting, and other calamities." The guide walked onward, continuing his presentation.

Michael saw a man apparently trying to take a selfie with the castle as a backdrop, and told Eve to wait just a second.

"Good morning," Michael said.

"Oh, hello."

"Can I give you a hand – take one for you? I think it would be easier to frame a good one."

"Thank you, so much. I'd like that."

Michael introduced himself. Eve watched as he took three or four photos from slightly different angles. The two chatted for a bit, then traded business cards, shook hands, and parted.

When he returned, she said, "Just happened to need a picture taken?"

"Sure. Just wanted to . . . You might as well know. I handed off the information we collected."

"You collected, actually, but I didn't see you give him anything. Other than your business card, that is."

"A memory card. You know, like you use in your camera or your phone. In the – on the back of the business card."

"Sneaky, but why not just send it from the ship. It would be faster."

"Maybe, but I don't know how secure the internet is on the ship, and this way, there isn't any electronic trail."

"Is it really all that sensitive? I mean you're getting into what seems like cloak and dagger stuff."

"I don't know if I'd go that far. But I don't know who is monitoring what on the ship's internet, and this is just safer. If the congressman has friends, I'd like it to be a little harder for any of them to connect us to the information."

"So, is that the end of our – your – job?"

"I guess it is. Unless I get a call to do more, that's about all I had to do."

"So, we can just enjoy the rest of the cruise? Seems a shame to waste a perfectly good river cruise."

"I couldn't agree with you more."

The tour of the castle took almost two hours. Eve thrilled at holding his hand, being a couple. Following the tour, everyone was loaded back onto the buses and driven back down the mountain to a bus park near the river. They had another two hours of shopping in Heidelberg.

They walked the streets in old Heidelberg. They stopped at the Lindt store and bought more chocolate than they thought they would ever need. "Maybe I can get Meg fat, too," quipped Eve.

"You're not fat," said Michael.

"When you work in fashion and have to wear all the things you create – and try to make them look the best they can, you have to be very self-conscious about every pound."

"Maybe we could do some more exercises."

She turned slowly and looked at him. "So – what did you have in mind?"

"Actually, not that, although at the rate we've been going, I'd guess a lot of calories have been burned off."

Having bought souvenirs as well as the chocolate, they walked back to the bus park, boarded the bus, and relaxed while they rode back to the ship. Once there, they decided on a light lunch and retired to their stateroom, where they napped in each other's arms.

Rested, Michael said he was going to go up onto the sundeck and exercise. Eve donned a pair of pale blue mid-thigh shorts and matching tank top and joined him.

"Just how am I supposed to concentrate on what I'm doing with you looking like that," he smiled.

"Just pay attention to what you're doing. Never

mind me," she said as she started stretching.

"Right, like that is even a possibility."

Eve straightened, turned and caught him staring at her derriere. "Just exercising your eyes isn't going to burn many calories," she said.

"Yeah, well, I told you that I could have trouble concentrating, then you – um – started stretching. I was intrigued by your . . ."

"By my what, sir?" she was trying her best to look disapproving, but in a few seconds, she broke out in laughter.

"Just for my information," he started, "are you trying to drive me absolutely wild?"

"Why Michael, I have no idea what you mean. How would I know you'd stare at me if I stretched my legs?"

By now, both were laughing.

Michael did a little stretching of his own, then began doing his Tai Chi forms.

Eve marveled at the smooth grace of his movements. It was a ballet, done slowly, beautifully.

"That is really beautiful," she said. "Could you teach me?"

"Well, I'm kind of a klutz, and I was able to learn it. But it took me some time. Once you have the moves, you can start perfecting them."

"Yours look perfect."

"Actually, I'm not even close. I took some lessons from a master. If you think this is good, you'd be watching him with your mouth open. That truly is a martial arts ballet."

He started to show her the moves. After about an hour, she was doing a semblance of the form.

"You're a quick study. I didn't learn what you have for weeks."

"Maybe it's the teacher."

"In this case, I'm sure it's the student."

"Let's see if we can do it together," she said.

They started together. The first time, he stood in front of her. She moved along with him. Next, they stood side by side. Before long, they were moving in unison.

"You're really great at this," he said, watching with awe her smooth and graceful moves.

"Maybe I should have mentioned the dance classes I took in college. This kind of brings it back. And, I love doing this with you." When she said it, she thought, *"You know, I really do love doing this with him."*

They were finally tired and decided to head to the bow of the ship. When they arrived, one of the lounge crew asked if they wanted anything, and they opted for mimosas. They sat in the open air of the sun deck, sipping their drinks, watching the sun head for the horizon.

"I'm really going to miss this when I have to return to the States and go back to work. Are very many of your assignments like this?"

"Once in a while. Not terribly often. Most are gathering information, then spending more time writing. Some assignments involve working – like being a guide, or working on a farm."

"It sounds fascinating."

"I'll be sure to include you when they want me to go back down into a coal mine."

"No thank you. That doesn't sound like much fun."

"Actually, it wasn't. I was supposed to get information on a company that was cutting corners on safety. So, when you are supposed to go down into a mine when you know there are safety violations, it just takes all the fun out of it."

"Can't you say 'no?' I mean you could die."

"You're allowed to turn down assignments once in a while, but if you do it frequently, they don't really need to have you around. They don't need anyone to take just cushy assignments."

"You mean like river cruises?"

"Are you kidding? They've put me on a boat from which I have no escape. I'm trapped in a stateroom with a beautiful woman who seems bent on wearing me out until I divulge all my secrets." He was laughing.

"I wouldn't say she was the only one who was trying to wear someone out," she said, laughing in return.

"Actually, this is the absolute best assignment I've ever had. And, thank you."

"Thank you. But if you hadn't convinced me to come along, who would have?"

"They'd probably paired me with Bertha Besqueezo – a short, dumpy, one-eyed, club footed Russian. The sex just wouldn't have been the same," he said it with a mock serious look on his face.

"God, you're terrible. If there is such a woman, she's probably sweet."

"Ex-KGB," now he was laughing. "They probably would have paired me with one of the assistants. And there are strict rules against – you know."

"So, you wanted to bring me along so you could – you know?"

"I wanted to bring you along because I wanted more of your company. I didn't assume – you know."

"Uh huh."

"Hey. It started with you rubbing my leg on the bus

tour of Strasbourg."

"No. It started with you doing that number on me with the sunscreen before I ever touched your leg. Don't try to lay this all on me."

"I couldn't resist. I was going to just put the sunscreen on, but when I felt how you were relaxing."

"You mean when you felt what was happening because of what you were doing."

"Okay. You win. Can we agree that there may be some 'responsibility' on each of us? Don't care if you lay it all at my feet, though. Best assignment. Ever. By far."

"I'm willing to take maybe a tiny bit of responsibility," she said with the look of innocence about her, "if after dinner, you would do to the rest of me what you did on the bus ride to my shoulders and upper back."

"Deal. Shall we?"

Twenty-seven

Eve opened her eyes slowly. Just as slowly, the ceiling of the stateroom came into focus. By tilting her gaze downward, she could see the dresser, closet, and large mirror at the end of the bed. To her right was the partition separating the bedroom, as such, from the bath and shower. Rolling her eyes to the left revealed that the heavy curtains were open and the sheers drawn closed to allow light, but not prying eyes, into the room. She turned her head just a bit and saw the ship was tied up about thirty feet from the shore, in this case a concrete wall, with a walkway. The ship was in the shade, and she supposed they were under a bridge.

Eve was naked under the sheet and duvet. She wasn't sure she wanted to move. The evening before, Michael had spent – *well*, she thought, *at least two hours* – performing a full body massage; from the top of her head all the way to the tips of her fingers and toes. He'd started very lightly, and as muscle layer after muscle layer had relaxed, his fingers – *strong fingers* – had probed ever deeper. At some point, she'd stopped even making noises and drifted off to some happy, dreamy place that she didn't want to leave right now. She vaguely remembered that as he'd finished massaging each side, he used a hot wash cloth to remove any excess oil. It had only increased the relaxation, and she'd remembered thinking, when she still could, that he could have poured her into a bottle.

She tested her legs. They moved, although with some effort. She was still very, very relaxed, some eight or ten hours later. Who knew? Who cared? Her arms felt the same. She noticed the room was quiet, and she assumed that Michael had gone elsewhere. Just at that time, the stateroom door opened and he entered.

"Well, there you are, sleepy head. Got to get up or you'll miss out on breakfast." He was wearing loose workout pants and a tank top, good-sized and well-defined muscles showing.

"I don't know if I can move. I think you doped me last night."

"Just a massage. I thought being able to do that would come in handy one day. Turns out, I was right."

She managed to roll on her side. It took some effort she was so relaxed. "Just where did you learn to do that?"

"A few years ago, they wanted to do a story about massage parlors and possible corruption, hanky-panky. You know. So, I was chosen to go to school to learn massage – then work undercover, so to speak, to find out what was going on. A lot of places were above board. A few used the opportunity to steal credit card numbers. Some were essentially brothels. A few provided kickbacks to the police. We even got a picture of one chief of police getting a happy ending as part of his reward."

"How long did all this take? The story, not the happy ending."

"About a year. I disappeared, and the story was published. A number of embarrassed people – especially in city councils and law enforcement."

"Especially one chief of police I imagine."

She managed to sit up and swing her legs to the floor. She took a towel from the night stand and wrapped herself in it before heading to the bath and shower. Ten minutes later, she emerged looking perfect, wearing white Bermuda shorts and a medium blue silk tank top.

They talked as they headed to the restaurant.

"I may be a bit wobbly from your, um, ministrations, sir."

"You're doing just fine. And, may I add, beautiful, as well."

"You're just saying that because, if I may be so bold, you're smitten. By the way, where are we?"

"Guilty, as charged, and we have docked in Koblenz. This is where the Rhine and Mosel rivers meet. There is a huge statue of Kaiser Wilhelm at the confluence. He was the first Kaiser Wilhelm and is credited with uniting a large number of small principalities into what became Germany. There is a castle to be toured, if you are interested."

"That sounds like fun, but as much as I would like to see it, I think I'd actually like to stay on the ship and just relax. I know it sounds stupid – I need to relax from all my relaxing – but if it would be okay . . ."

"Of course. Relax alone, or would you like company

for your relaxation?"

"I'd love to have your company, but I don't want to keep you from seeing the castle."

"I'd rather do anything with you. My apartment may not be seven hundred years old, but it is cold and drafty, so what's the big deal?" he said with a laugh.

They arrived at the tail end of breakfast. Eve ordered tea, a small omelet, and toast.

"So, I guess you don't want me to tell you about the chocolate museum just a hundred feet or so up the quay."

"You've got to be kidding me – right?"

"Nope. Chocolate museum. Just up there." He pointed toward the bow of the ship.

"I don't know if I can resist, and I just shouldn't."

"If you don't stop saying things like that, I'm going to have to spank you."

Eve cocked one eye and looked at Michael. She raised her hand to catch the server's eye and said, "Two champagnes, please." Then, she looked at Michael and said, "We'll put on some music. Looks like we've got ourselves an event."

After breakfast, they walked to reception and picked up their re-boarding passes before heading off to the chocolate museum. After an hour, they returned to the ship with yet more chocolate and holed up in their room until lunch.

They ate light at lunch – both opting for salads and cod filet. After lunch, they headed for the sun deck where they spent time sitting in the sun and relaxing – talking as the mood struck.

"So," said Eve, "what after this? I mean, will you get another assignment right away, or is there a brief respite, not that anyone really needs a respite after this."

"Not sure. Usually, there is a period between assignments, but like you say, I'm not sure a rest period is needed after this. It depends where and when the next story is. I suppose after a story like this, they'll probably send me into some war zone."

She looked at him with a sense of concern. "You're kidding. Right? They wouldn't really send you into a war zone."

"Don't know. Hard to tell. There's always someplace where the government is killing people and trying to keep it quiet, or where the government is taking money from criminals to turn a blind eye. Be hard to get up for that one after this." He took her hand.

Suddenly, there was an emptiness inside her. And, a little sickness. She wanted this fairy tale to last. She wanted the time with him to last. And, all of a sudden, there was a realization that it really would come to an end. She took her hand from his, stood, and walked to the railing. She was staring at the river flowing by when he came to her side.

"First, I want to tell you that this has been a magical time," he started. "I'd love for this never to end, but we know you can't stay with me in Paris. You've got a business to run. And my life, well, my life is this. Usually a lot worse than this. Can we try to enjoy the last few days we have together? Maybe we can figure . . ." His sentence trailed off.

She sat for a long time, thinking about him and their possible future. "I'm sorry, but I need to ask – about your, well, about your past. If all Digby's have a – a tragic event, what was yours? Please."

Michael stared, then, "It's something I want to keep buried."

"Ghosts have a way of coming back when you least want them to. Trust me, I know." She thought about her own, private ghost. "I'd really like to know – and help."

"I'm not sure you can."

"You have to give me a chance. A woman?"

He sat for a long time. His eyes narrowed for a while, a look she didn't like was on his face. Then, his face softened and was sad. He said, "Yes."

"And, she betrayed you."

"Yes. And let's leave it at that." He got up and walked away.

Twenty-eight

The next morning, the ship docked in Cologne, or as the Germans spell it, Koln. After breakfast, they joined the rest of the passengers for a walk to the cathedral. They learned it had been started in the thirteenth century but hadn't been finished until the late eighteen hundreds. There were also ruins of a Roman road, although the guide noted that in rehabilitating the road, the stones were removed, and original positions marked in chalk. With a rain, the marks and original positions were lost. Now, he'd said, "it is just a lumpy road. And much worse than what the Romans did." In all, Cologne was an interesting city. Michael and Eve were lost in a sadness that came from their earlier realization that the trip would end and they would depart for their separate lives.

In the evening, they embarked on a dinner and beer-tasting tour. The food was traditional German. The beer, Kolsch, was served cold in a small glass. Their tour guide explained that some Germans made fun of the small portions, however, he'd said, "In Munich, you get a great big stein of beer. By the time you're half-way through it, you have flat, warm beer. In Koln, your beers are smaller, but they are cold and fresh." The beer was also very mild, which both Michael and Eve appreciated. After the tour, they stayed in the town square, sipping a wine, enjoying the evening and each other's company – a bit of the sadness lifted if only in the realization that they should try to enjoy the time they had left together.

"Do you ever get to choose what you want to do for your next assignment?"

"Sometimes. If something comes up that looks interesting, you can ask if you can pursue it. Sometimes – just like the rest of life – the answer is yes. Sometimes no."

"So, I don't suppose they'd let you do an exclusive story about an up and coming fashion house in the U.S."

He looked at her, then down at the table, then back at her. "I've already done one."

"Which one?"

"Yours."

"Ours? You mean Eve-M Fashions? Why haven't I – we ever seen it?"

"You have. It was in Fashion Week."

"Wait. No. That was done by . . ."

"Anastasia Rose."

"Yes. Anastas . . . but we talked to her. It was a she – a woman."

"A female assistant asked some pretty standard questions. That information was given to me. I did additional research and wrote an article. Actually, the writing of the article was ordered from above. The boss wanted an article about Eve-M and I was tasked with providing one. Turns out your business does some really great things, and writing a good article was easy. I wrote the article and sent it up the chain."

"But that article started us on our way to success. It – oh my – it brought John and Meg back together again after fifteen years. They're married because of that article."

"Yes. John is a good friend. I didn't know his whole story. Guys don't often talk about troubled pasts. I was surprised at where the article was published. Not one of our magazines, but then I guess editors and publishers have friends. When the article was shown to John, he fairly flew – pardon the pun – back to the States. He had no idea how he was going to reconnect with the young lady – Meg. He just said it was the most important thing he ever had to do."

Eve was just staring.

"But – it does make one," said Michael, "in this case me being the one, wonder just who controls our lives. It's just so weird that – if you look at it this way – was to make your business famous enough that John could reconnect. Not that your business isn't great. It's just that – I don't even know how to say what I'm feeling."

"I know the feeling," said Eve. "Here I thought the article was 'just' good luck – you know, a fashion reporter who happened to see and like our stuff. And wrote an article. I don't know if this other makes me wonder about life and who might be watching."

"I've seen this sort of thing happen before. Always with a, forgive the term, happy ending. Like serendipity with a push. Somebody looking out and trying to make lives better."

"Still, in a way," continued Eve, "wouldn't you want to control your own destiny?"

"Maybe it's just the illusion of control. John and Meg seem to be very, very happy for two people whose lives may have had a push. Maybe it is a way of balancing out what should have been before."

Eve wanted to say something, but she was unable. *I feel like a college freshman trying to figure out a conundrum that the professor threw out.*

"I don't suppose whoever is doing this would like to figure out a – now, forgive my use of the term – happy ending for us," she said.

"One can only hope, and wonder what that might look like. However, my guess is that if we're to have a happy ending, we'll have to figure it out for ourselves."

They walked back to the ship, holding hands, enjoying a warm, beautiful night in Koln.

Twenty-nine

They were sitting alone at a table for breakfast, enjoying their meal. Eve was in white shorts and a short-sleeved blouse. Michael wore khaki slacks and a white shirt. The day was sunny. The ship had just slipped the mooring and was headed to Kinderdijk, the last stop before Amsterdam.

Frank Smith was at the next table. Missy was not present; likely still asleep in the stateroom. *Maybe*, thought Michael, *she's had her fill of him.* There were three other people at Frank's table. He was talking about seeing the windmills at Kinderdijk – which he pronounced as kinder dick, with a snicker each time he said it.

"Imagine, if you will, having a place that's named after children's, well, penises."

Michael couldn't listen to any more. He leaned toward their table and said, "I believe it is pronounced kinder dyke. One of the reasons is thought to be that the children built this particular dyke, hence, children's dyke."

Frank looked at Michael with a slight scowl, then smiled, "Well, they should have spelled it more correctly. Besides, it's a bit more salacious," he winked at one of the women at his table, "when you say kinder dick." Apparently proud of himself, he smiled, sat back and puffed out his chest, which almost came to the level of his belly.

Eve leaned over to Michael and whispered, "Don't even

try. He's a pig."

"You'll give pigs a bad name," he returned.

A crewman entered the restaurant with a ten by twelve manila envelope. He walked to Frank's table and cleared his throat.

Frank turned and looked at him. "Yes?"

"This envelope came aboard for you early this morning." The crewman handed the envelope to Frank. Frank scowled again, perhaps wondering who was sending him envelopes during his vacation.

Michael was wondering how many people knew about him even being here.

Frank continued talking to the other passengers, but his curiosity finally got the better of him. He tore the flap and started to pull out the contents – never stopping his monologue. He looked down at the papers pulled part-way out and his face turned white. His jaw dropped open. He tried to stuff the contents back into the envelope and stood up rapidly, knocking his chair over.

"Oh, my God! Oh, my God! Oh, my God!"

He ran to the front of the restaurant, his belly and jowls bouncing as he ran. "Oh, my God! Oh, my God! Oh, my God!"

"I'm not one hundred percent sure," said Michael, "but I don't think that whatever is in that envelope is good news."

"Watching this," said Eve smiling, "might have made the whole trip worthwhile – you know, on top of the food, sex, massage, and scenery."

Frank kept running back and forth, all the time repeating, "Oh, my God! Oh, my God! Oh, my God!" Then, he said, "Oh, my God! There'll be reporters in Kinder dick. I've got to get off this boat!" He ran past his former table, the other passengers sitting with their mouths open. He picked up the envelope and started to run to the exit, dropping the envelope as he did.

Michael got out of his chair and calmly walked to where the envelope lay. He picked it up and returned to where Eve was sitting. He opened the flap and pulled out a British tabloid. On the front were three of the pictures that Michael had taken on the boat – showing Frank perfectly, and in one practically naked in his stateroom, while the identifying features of Missy had been fuzzed out. The headline in huge letters read, **US Congressman on love tryst cruise with minor**.

"Well, there you go," said Michael. "They say no publicity is bad publicity, but I can see why he might have taken this badly. Good pictures, though."

Eve shook her head. "I don't think this is going to get him re-elected. Even if she isn't really a minor. So, is this considered a subtle approach?"

"About as subtle as a shovel to the back of the head. We'd better go see if we can stop him from doing something stupid."

"Yes. He said something about reporters at Kinderdijk. And getting off the boat. You don't suppose?"

"Let's go." He handed Eve the envelope and said, "Here, hide this in your bag."

And with that, they left the restaurant and went up one level to the lounge. Frank was just finishing the third of three triple whiskeys.

Michael tried to talk with him. "Frank, are you okay? It seems like you're upset. Can we help?"

Frank looked at Michael, then Eve, and again said, "Oh, my God! Oh, my God! There'll be reporters in Kinder dick. I've got to get off this boat!" He rushed past Michael and pushed Eve out of his way. Eve lifted her arms and shrugged her shoulders. Frank headed up one level to the sun deck. Michael started after him.

On the sun deck, Frank continued to run back and forth, then, he headed aft. It took Michael a minute to locate Frank. When he did, Michael started walking slowly toward him, not wanting to further upset a man apparently at wit's end.

Then, Frank started toward the rail at the far back of the ship. He was looking around frantically. Other passengers were starting to back away from him, men shielding women, putting themselves between Frank and their loved ones.

Michael figured out, too late, what Frank was going to do. In a second, Frank's thick form was straddling the railing. Then, he plunged over the side and into the Rhine.

Michael ran to the railing and looked over, seeing Frank sputtering in the swirling current and bobbing up and down. He cursed and put one leg over the railing, gauging the twenty-five-foot drop to the water below. He started to swing his other leg over the railing when he felt a strong arm around his waist. He was pulled back and thrown to the deck.

It took a few seconds for Michael to catch his breath and come out of the daze. He looked over and saw Eve lying beside him, her arm still around his waist. "Oh no you don't, mister," she said. "Not in a million years am I going to lose you that way."

Slowly, Michael rolled over and got to his knees. He stood, looked at her and said, "You win. I'm not going in." He walked to the railing and looked into the river. Only brown swirling water was visible. He scanned the bank, seeing nothing. The ship was stopping, or rather keeping with the current. A small boat was launched.

Thirty

The captain took charge of the rescue, or more likely, recovery efforts and had turned over ship maneuvering to the first officer who kept the ship stationary in the current – moving down the river at the same rate as the water. If the man who went overboard surfaced, he should come up right where the ship was. A small boat that was launched went back and forth, searching both the river banks and around the ship for an hour, without success. It would be three days before Frank's bloated body would be found some eight miles downriver.

Michael and Eve sat on the sun deck.

"I can't believe he did that," she said. "I mean, until he actually went over the side, it was kind of comical – him running back and forth, sputtering. Then, boom. It all changed."

"Yeah. You're right. It was kind of funny. I don't think he had a chance in the river. I don't think the captain believes it, either."

"And you, you idiot, thinking you were going to save him. If you'd have jumped, we'd be looking for two bodies right now, and I would have been – I'd have been a wreck."

Michael had tried to get the captain's attention for the last forty-five minutes, to no avail. When he would try to speak to him, the captain would wave him off saying what he was attending to had to take precedence over everything else.

Finally, when it looked like the recovery was winding down, he again approached the captain. "Sir. Have some information that I believe is important not only for you, but for the company, as well."

"Okay Mister . . ."

"Franklin, George Franklin, sir."

"Okay, Mister Franklin, what is this information that you believe is so important."

"We should go somewhere private, sir."

The captain looked at Michael and gave a sigh of resignation. The look on his face indicated that he didn't believe the information was important or so important to require privacy. "The restaurant will be closed. We can go there."

When they entered the restaurant, the chef and wait staff were setting up for lunch.

"Could we please have total privacy, sir? I believe you'll understand in a few minutes."

The captain went to the chef and said a few words. As he returned to the table, the chef started ushering all of the staff from the restaurant.

"I hope this doesn't take too long," said the captain. "While everything looks like it runs perfectly and smoothly, the crew works very hard to keep things on schedule."

"Yes, sir. We understand. This shouldn't take long. Eve, could I have the envelope, please?"

Eve reached into her bag and produced the manila envelope.

"This is what Mister Smith received just before he started running around the ship. He also started saying, over and over, that he had to get off the ship before it reached Kinderdijk."

Michael pulled the tabloid from the envelope and handed it to the captain. The captain looked at it, not understanding at first what was so important.

"It would seem that Mr. Smith was in reality a United States congressman, sir. A United States congressman leaped off the boat and into the river."

With that explanation, the captain turned white. Not only had he lost a passenger, but it appeared he had lost a very important passenger. One that would make the company, the ship, and him, look bad.

"Oh, no. This is terrible. How could such a thing happen. We take such care."

"Yes, sir. However, the bad news isn't quite over. Not only was the congressman traveling under a false name, as the article says, he was traveling with a girl. Not his wife. Together. In the same stateroom."

"Oh, no. This is so bad. Even if they left the ship in

Amsterdam – together and in good health. But, at least no one would know. Now – now, oh my God. This is the end of my career."

"That's why I wanted to talk to you – in private. I think the damage can be minimized. Not completely erased, but I think there is a way."

The captain looked at him, "What do you mean? I can't lie. There will be an inquiry. The authorities. The company."

"And, I don't want you to lie." The captain looked a bit relieved, but not much. "If you hadn't seen this paper, who would you say fell from the ship and into the river?"

"Mr. Smith. Mr. Frank Smith," said the captain.

"That's right. And if you hadn't seen this paper, which, by the way, you have no way of knowing is or isn't legitimate, you would still believe that to be true."

"I'm listening."

"So, as far as you are concerned, it was Frank Smith that jumped ship - trying to swim ashore before we reached Kinderdijk. That's also what your records will show. You need not mention anything about a congressman."

The captain thought that over for a minute or two. "Fine. There is no real lie in any of that. What about when it is discovered that he was a congressman?"

"By then, the story should be back in the U. S. They're not going to focus as much on his death on this ship as they are on him traveling under an assumed name with a woman who is not his wife. Nobody likes a good scandal better than the good and righteous people of the United Sates."

"What about the girl? It is bound to come out that she was not his wife."

"Why? I suggest that my wife take the lady, they've already met and chatted, to see the windmills in Kinderdijk. While they are doing that, perhaps the young lady's things could be moved to another room – if there is one. The authorities may want to look through his – Frank Smith's – things. We can tell the young lady what happened. Later, In Amsterdam, where there are professionals who can deal with such things, she can be given grief counselling."

As the captain seemed to mull this over, Eve was thinking, *He's pretty good at this. And it is really complicated. I wonder how he managed to put all this together so fast.*

"Okay," the captain finally said. "I'll get the purser and we can go over this again. Would you be willing to explain it to him, as well?"

"Yes. I think that is best."

"Good. I need to get back to navigating and docking the ship."

The captain went to the entrance of the restaurant and called to the purser, who was at his desk, one deck below. After introductions were made, the captain headed to the bridge and Michael explained everything to the purser.

Eve walked to the 'Smith' stateroom and knocked on the door. After a bit, Missy answered.

"He isn't here," she said. "He wanted to get breakfast, and I wanted to sleep in."

"That's okay, honey, I think he's going to be busy for a while. I was wondering, would you like to come with me when I visit the windmills?"

"Oh, that would be super! When do we get there? Do you think he will be upset?"

"I think it will be fine. Why don't we look for something for you to wear? I'll bet you've got some really cute things. Let's see. Okay?

With that, Missy started pulling out clothes and checking for cute matches.

Thirty-one

With Eve's help and direction, Missy decided on a pair of faded blue jeans, white long-sleeved blouse, and a pair of Keds originals. Since it was going to be a 'girl's day,' Eve suggested they wear minimal makeup, and did Missy's hair in a pony tail. Eve dressed casually, as well. The result was that Missy now appeared to be about twelve years old, which suited Eve. In the event there were any reporters in Kinderdijk, she wanted it to look like a mother-daughter outing.

Michael watched as they walked up the ramp and through a group of what could be reporters standing about on the quay. No one payed any attention to the two women. Michael turned and headed for the congressman's stateroom. He knocked and the purser opened the door.

"Yes?"

"I thought that I might give you a hand. It will go a lot faster, and two pairs of eyes will be better than one."

The purser thought about that for a minute. When he looked like he might not accept Michael's help, he slid past him and into the room.

"Do you want me to start out here," he asked, "or in the bathroom?"

Resigned, the purser finally replied, "I had started in the bathroom. Why don't you start gathering things out here?"

Michael acknowledged him, and when the purser stepped around the corner and into the bathroom, Michael reached up and removed the small, hidden camera he had placed. He slid it into his pocket, then, he started looking through the items on the built-in chest of drawers at the foot of the bed. A case for carrying two bottles of wine was sitting on the top of the drawers. Michael's eye was drawn to it because of the odd design. There appeared to be small black smooth stones set into the leather around the circumference at the top. When he looked closer, he found that at least one wasn't what it seemed.

"Hey. Come look at this."

The purser, looking somewhat put out, left the bathroom and joined him. "What?"

"This wine carrier. At least one of the stones doesn't look right." Michael opened the carrier to find that this was indeed a lens, connected to a camera and a digital storage disk. "Nice. It would appear that the – and I hesitate to use the word – gentleman, was recording what happened here." Michael was pointing to the bed. "Videos, probably so he could relive the experience later."

"This is unbelievable," said the purser. "I'm glad you found that. Can you imagine what that would cause if the wrong people got hold of whatever is on the disk?"

"Maybe they should. And find out just what he was."

"Yes, but it certainly wouldn't reflect well on the company – or this ship. We try to do everything right. We shouldn't be punished, or reputation tarnished, because of someone like this."

"I guess you're right. There's no telling what else might be in here. Do you think it would be possible to move the girl – lady – into another stateroom?"

The purser thought for a moment. "Yes, there is one just two doors down. Actually, a little more luxurious than this one. We could move her there."

"There's no telling what else might be in this room, and it would be nice for you to have the luxury of more time. Besides, the authorities . . ."

"Yes, you're right. We can gather the young lady's things and move them."

Michael looked around the room. There wasn't a lot. What caught his eye was a teddy bear on the nightstand on what he assumed was Missy's side of the bed. A cute little bear, wearing a tuxedo. He wondered if it was a gift. He went over and picked up. It was a little heavier than he thought it would be. He looked at it more closely and said nothing to the purser.

Within forty minutes, all of Missy's things had been moved to the other stateroom. Waiting for the return of the two women, Michael went to the lounge and ordered a scotch.

Thirty-two

Eve and Missy had returned to the ship. Eve had explained what 'Frank' had done. *Missy took it surprisingly well*, she thought. Missy actually seemed more relieved than upset, which Eve thought showed she wasn't really all that enamored of the congressman. Because they still had to pack up and send his things back after the authorities reviewed the case, they had moved her into a slightly better cabin.

Michael, Eve, and Missy all attended the daily briefing together. The cruise director went over the schedule for the following morning. Suitcases had to be placed into the hallway by specific times, depending on the departure time from the ship. There was no mention of the 'accident.' Missy seemed somewhat confused; likely Frank was going to attend to the details. Either that, or Missy really didn't know what time they were to leave – or where they were to go. Luckily, the purser had copies of the guests' itineraries. As it turned out, Missy and Frank were to have left Amsterdam on different flights. Frank's was direct to Washington, DC, and Missy was to connect through London. The flights were on different airlines.

"Nice," said Michael. "It will look like they came from two completely different destinations. And get this. He's flying first class. She's flying coach."

"It's really too bad he drowned," said Eve. "He really deserved to suffer a lot more than he did. He'll probably get some kind of a hero's funeral – accidental death of this great congressman while on a – what do you think they will call it, a fact-finding trip?"

"Probably, although there may be some information leaked to members of his party that will make them consider a much less grandiose send off. Oh, yeah, I found a camera."

"You found . . ."

"A camera. The congressman had a hidden camera pointed at the bed. He was apparently recording their, um, sessions so that he could relive the experience later."

"How?"

"He had a faux wine bottle carrier on the top of the drawers. The design was weird, so I took a closer look and found a lens. When I opened the 'wine carrier,' there was the camera and recording disk."

"Oh my God! This just can't get any worse. What did you do?"

"I turned the wine carrier, camera, and disk over to the purser. I think he and the captain will discuss it. They may watch just enough to make sure what it is, then, who knows? Oh yes, it can get worse."

"No. Now what?"

"Sure you want to know?"

"No, but in for a penny, in for a pound. Tell me. Please. I think."

"Well, as the saying goes, once I tell you, I can't un-tell you. I found another camera and recording."

"Another one?"

"Yes. This one was in a teddy bear on what I believe was Missy's side of the bed. The teddy was wearing a tuxedo. When I picked it up, it felt heavy. So, I investigated. There was a lens where one of the buttons should have been and it led to a recording device and disk. The position of the teddy was such that it would record anything reflected in the mirror."

"Oh my God! Do you think he gave her the bear?"

"Actually, I think it was her bear. I think she was getting some insurance, you know, just in case."

"This can't get worse." After a minute, she asked, "What did you do?"

"I got the disk and ran a bit of it in my laptop. Just enough to see what might be on it."

Eve was staring.

"I saw enough to know that it was positioned to record the reflections, and enough to see that it was Missy doing the positioning of the bear so it would record that way."

"I think I'm going to be sick."

"Yeah, it is pretty incredible. I think there have been major motion pictures made without as many cameras as there were in that stateroom."

"True as that is, it really isn't funny. Where is the bear and the disk?"

"She's got the bear. With a blank disk. I stole hers. If nothing else, it will keep her from blackmailing the family. Insurance is one thing . . ."

"But wait," said Eve, "how do you know you didn't appear in the movies – you know, when you were in their stateroom?"

"Well, for one, I have her disk. And, I was able to check his disk. He apparently had to turn the camera on manually. It wasn't on when I was there."

"I need a drink."

"Champagne?"

"No. Three fingers of whiskey."

"Yeah. Nothing like true love."

Thirty-three

The ship docked in Amsterdam, and the passengers began their orderly departure. The purser said he would take care of Missy. They learned later that he had moved her off the ship with the crew. Any waiting reporters would have been disappointed.

Michael and Eve left at mid-morning. Michael had gotten reservations for a hotel in the old section of Amsterdam for two nights.

"Are you sure you can stay another couple of nights?" he asked.

"It's the least I can do, considering everything you've done for me. After all, I was saved from who knows what in Paris, had a river cruise, almost got killed by a moving bridge, was involved in a lot of cloak and dagger stuff, and found out an innocent young girl wasn't quite as innocent as I'd thought. This is not how I thought this week would go when I thought of it a month or so ago."

"Disappointed?"

"Pretty much only in the part where I found out little miss innocent wasn't as innocent as I thought."

Michael had a funny look in his eyes. Finally, the look cleared.

"You okay? She asked.

"Yeah. Just a . . . Never mind."

Michael had booked two nights at the Pestana Amsterdam Riverside. The rooms were modern and good sized. Eve was pleased with the choice.

After a good night's sleep, they had breakfast, then set out. They did a canal boat tour and visited the Anne Frank House, after which they had a somber lunch, thinking about the young girl who had come so close to escaping the Nazis. They visited the Van Gogh museum and Vondelpark.

They'd decided on a light dinner, and headed for a small restaurant. On the way, they stopped by the Café' Pollux. There was a television on in the bar. The news was on. Michael started to sip his beer, then dropped his glass on the table.

"What?" Eve started to say.

Michael pointed to the television. On the screen was Missy, accompanied by an attorney. The script running under the picture stated that she was suing the family of the late congressman who had practically forced her to go to Europe with him so he could have a tryst with a young woman where he wouldn't be found. It was only by chance that she had suffered a spontaneous abortion and lost the child that he had created with her.

Michael left the café and went out onto the street. He was leaning against a tree when Eve got to him.

"I – I can't believe she is doing this," he said. "We went to such great lengths to protect her. And, she outs herself in an effort to – what, essentially blackmail the family. This is . . ."

Eve tried to put her arm around him. "I don't know what she thinks she's doing. This can't be any good. Not for anybody. She's . . ."

But something had changed in him. Something had snapped. He pushed her arm away. "This is just . . ." he started. "She deliberately lied. She is lying now – just to . . ." He wasn't finishing any of his sentences.

"The congressman was a pig," started Eve. "He didn't deserve . . ."

Michael turned. There was more than anger on his face. Rage. For the first time, Eve was frightened. "That little bitch! It isn't what his family deserved. She's lying about – about having his child so she can blackmail the family. That lying, cheating, worthless . . ."

"Michael," Eve said. But Michael wasn't listening.

"You want to know about my past? Yeah. A woman. A woman I loved – trusted. Married. I was happy to give her everything she wanted. She announced she was pregnant. I was thrilled. I had everything I wanted in life. Then, there were tests. The doctors thought the baby might have a problem."

"Oh, no!" said Eve.

Michael held up his hand. "They ran tests. One of the tests showed I couldn't have been the baby's father. I confronted her – devastated. She said she'd never loved me – only pretended. For money – things. She'd been having sex with this other man for months. Now, she was going to get an abortion and a lawyer, claim I made her do it and that I was abusive. She would take me for everything I ever worked for. You wanted to know my past? That's my past. Betrayed doesn't even start to cover it."

"Michael."

But he turned and walked off. Eve stood in disbelief.

Thirty-four

The phone rang three times before Eve heard Meg pick up. It was Eleven o'clock in the morning.

"Oh, Meg," she began. "I don't know what happened. One minute we seemed to be happy, the next, it seemed like he was crazy. Mad. More than mad. I was actually frightened. I didn't know what to say or do."

"Slow down, Eve. Tell me exactly what happened."

Over the next twenty minutes, Eve told Meg about the congressman getting the paper. How he ran around the ship like a chicken with his head cut off, until he finally – literally – jumped ship, to his death. She told about going to see the windmills with Missy and what Michael had found in the stateroom. Missy had gotten shipped off, and they thought that would be the end of it, with her identity protected.

"Then, we stopped by a café for a drink before dinner," Eve said through the sobs. "And there on TV, was Missy, claiming that she had been forced to go to Europe with this man, who used a false name. She said she'd gotten pregnant by him and suffered a spontaneous abortion. She has an attorney and is going to sue the family. That's when Michael went nuts. I tried to comfort him, but it was no use. He wandered off into the night. I didn't know what to do, so I went back to the hotel."

"Oh, Eve," said Meg. "I'm so sorry."

"Sometime in the middle of the night, I heard the door open. I thought he's settled down and we would talk about it in the morning. A little while later, I heard the door open again, and when I got up and looked around, all of his things were gone. I don't know where he went or if he's even okay."

"It's going to be okay, Eve. Really." Eve heard Meg yell, "JOHN! I NEED YOU – NOW!"

"Okay, Eve, I'm going to tell John just what you told me. I'm going to put you on speaker so if I get anything wrong, you correct me. Okay? Hang in there, baby. We're here for you."

Over the next few minutes, Meg briefed John. Her monologue was only briefly interrupted by occasional sobbing from Eve.

After hearing Meg's brief, Eve heard John say, "Crap!" Then he said, "Okay, Eve. What I'm about to tell you doesn't excuse Michael for what he did, but at least you'll be able to understand what he's going through and why." For the next ten minutes, John told Eve what had happened to Michael – his wife, the betrayal, and the threats. And, likely, how Missy's behavior had triggered the same response.

Eve was still sobbing. "He told me that, but I'm not – I'm not going to betray him. I love him. Oh God. I love him."

"What he's feeling isn't about you. It's about someone he loved and trusted who betrayed him badly. It's about being afraid to love – really love – because it not only opens old wounds, it presents the possibility for being hurt very badly again. I don't think he would have reacted that way unless he was afraid of opening himself up to hurt and betrayal. Stupid as it sounds, he reacted that way because he loves you and is afraid."

"So, what do I do?"

"When is your flight?" asked Meg.

"Two days from now. I'll send you the information. I'm going to London. I can't stay here." Eve was still crying.

Meg asked if Eve wanted her to come there.

"No. I'll be fine. Well, maybe not fine, but I'll get by until I'm home."

They cut the connection.

Thirty-five

Michael turned off the street and walked into his apartment building. The lobby felt cool after walking from the Metro in the afternoon sun. He heard laughter in the elevator above and decided to take the stairs. He didn't feel like laughter. In a few minutes, he arrived at the door to his apartment and searched his pockets for his keys. He found them and paused before putting the key into the first lock. The last time he was here, it was a happier time. He had spent the night with Eve, and they set out on an adventure together. Now, he was returning home to an empty apartment with an empty, dead feeling inside.

Michael swung the door open. Sunlight bathed the inside of the apartment. He saw the sofa had been turned. Now, the back was against the large window. The two overstuffed chairs and coffee table were in the same places as before. The conversation group facing the interior of the apartment rather than the street scene out the window. An old fashion glass sat on a marble coaster on the walnut table. In it were an inch or so of a brown liquid and a single ice cube. John Kelly sat in the overstuffed chair at the far end of the table.

"Long way to come to rearrange furniture," started Michael.

"Your Feng Shui was all wrong. The energy couldn't flow. It was blocked. Block your energy, and your entire life might be screwed up. You should know that. By the way, there's a package on the table for you."

Michael walked to the table. There was a manila envelope, containing a box. He opened the envelope, then, the box. The two rings Eve had worn on the trip were inside, padded by cotton. There was a note. 'We parted before I could return these to you. Thank you for loaning them to me. I enjoyed wearing them – and pretending. Always, Eve.' A giant's hand was crushing Michael's heart. After a minute, when he could trust himself to speak, he turned.

"You know, you're not supposed to dilute the scotch. It's a sin. A mortal sin."

"That's not true. In Edinburgh they tell you that a bit of water or a single small ice cube brings out the flavor of the drink."

Michael stared.

"But, if you want, we can talk about furniture arrangements and the best way to enjoy a glass of Scotch – or, we can talk about what's really important."

"Like?"

"What do you mean – 'like?' Eve. You and Eve."

Michael looked down. His whole being deflated. "Well, we all knew that couldn't . . ."

"Nobody knew but you. Everybody else, including Eve, hoped you'd buried the past."

"How did you find out about . . ."

"Jesus, Michael. I'm married to her best friend. Do you think that when you put a stake through Eve's heart she was just going to go off and sulk? Well, she did, but she also needed comfort and understanding. She called Meg. And, by the way, I care a lot about Eve, as well."

"So, I'm an ass."

"Ass is nicer than I was going to say, but yeah, for now we can go with ass. You think every woman is Clarabelle. Waiting to take you for a ride."

"Merrilee, John, her name was Merrilee. Clarabelle was a cow on a kid's TV show."

"Merrilee, Clarabelle, whatever. That's not Eve. You should know that."

"I know, it's just that . . ."

"It's what?"

"I can't imagine that anyone like Eve would . . ."

"What?"

"I'm nothing. I don't deserve someone like her. She could never . . ."

"She could never what, Michael? She could never love you? Why not?"

"I realized, after Merrilee, that no one would ever really love me. Maybe the things I could buy. Maybe the money I could make. But never just me."

"You're kidding. Eve adores you – you – not your money, even if she knew you had some. Not your lavish lifestyle." As he said the word 'lifestyle,' John waved his hand around the small apartment. "YOU!"

"You couldn't understand."

"Because all that happened to me was to fall in love with a woman, get shot, convicted of murder and sent to Europe for fifteen years? Then, to come back and confess that I met her on purpose and was paid as a bodyguard. Yes, I can see why I could never understand."

"And by the way," John continued, "Clarabelle . . ."

"Merrilee."

"Whatever. She tried the same scam again. It's not YOU. She's the pathological one."

"What do you mean?"

"She tried the same scam on another guy. Picked another guy with money – she didn't like him, but he was going to fund her lifestyle. He had money and friends. Took the kids away from her – he didn't know about the first one, by the way. Pretty much destroyed her life. She's in North Dakota now. Spends her days in a packing plant making minimum wage and her nights slurping beers. If that guy hadn't caught on and stopped her, she'd have a whole string by now. All women aren't like that."

"How do you know this? You could be lying."

"Why? You could check it yourself."

"Still, guys like me – we, they . . ."

"Don't deserve to be loved? Eve loves you, Michael. It's the truth. You know it is, even if you don't believe it yet. Eve loves you, and she is hurting. You should do something about that. Before it's too late. You saved her – twice. Now it's her turn to save you. But you have to let her in."

"Save me?"

"Yes. Save you. From that hollow feeling inside every time you think about not having someone to love. From the belief that every woman is like what's her name. From your belief that you aren't worthy of love."

"I . . ."

"It could be your last chance to stop living in pain and hatred." John knocked back the scotch, got up, and walked to the door. "Good luck, Michael. It's time to choose. Love or loneliness." John left and closed the door quietly behind him.

Thirty-six

There were crowds and lines, as is usual at Heathrow. Still, it was better than flying out of Paris. That airport was notorious for delays and problems. Eve had a Club World ticket – business class. It came with perks. As she worked her way through the stringent security, Eve thought, *Not enough perks, but I guess this is modern air travel.*

Boarding was delayed by about ten minutes, a last minute 'issue.' Eve had to smile. With the British, a major catastrophe was usually described as an 'issue.' The end of the world would likely be a 'slight problem.'

Boarding began, Club World boarded first. They might have boarded First Class, but not all BA planes had a First-Class section. She'd heard that BA First Class was basically a small apartment – with all the amenities. Club World, she thought, was good enough. Your seat was in a small cubicle, and the seat reclined and extended to connect with a foot rest – essentially making a bed. And, of course, you were treated like royalty.

"Thank you, Miss Belot. Welcome to your flight."

"Thank you." Eve collected her ticket and passport and walked down the jetway. The flight attendant looked at her ticket and directed her up the left aisle toward the front of the aircraft. Her seat was right behind the forward bulkhead. Her ticket indicated she would be on the left side of the aisle, one seat from the window. That suited her. She was tired and wanted to rest. Besides, after takeoff there wasn't going to be much to see. She looked at her watch – *forty minutes until departure - then, six hours until I'm – home.* She missed home, but there was no joy in her words.

A few people were already seated, she noticed, as she walked up the aisle. Other passengers were putting away bags in the overhead. The passenger in the seat across the aisle from hers had his blanket over him, turned away, trying to sleep already.

Eve put her carry-on in the overhead and sat in her seat. As was the luck of the draw, her seat faced backwards. Every other seat did. It made all the cubicles and 'beds' fit. The flight attendant greeted her and handed her a glass – a real glass – of champagne. As she took her first sip, Eve saw a flight attendant walking up the aisle, carrying a dozen beautiful red roses. *Wonder who the lucky girl is*, she thought. *Probably one of the flight attendants a pilot wants to boink. A gift, to seal the deal. God, I've gotten cynical in the last couple of days.*

The flight attendant stopped at her seat. Eve looked around, wondering who was getting the flowers.

"These are for you Ma'am," the flight attendant said.

"Maybe you have the wrong seat."

"No, Ma'am. No mistake."

"But I don't . . ."

A man's voice came from across the aisle. "Please,

he must want to apologize for something terrible that he's done."

Eve looked to see the passenger in the seat across had rolled over. It was Michael. He got out of his chair and took the roses. He handed them to her and said, "This is a partial apology for being such an ass."

"You weren't . . ."

"Yes, I was a complete ass. You may never forgive me, but I have to at least apologize. It is important even if you never want to see me again. I'm sorry. There is no, 'I'm sorry, but' – but you do deserve an explanation. I am an engineer. What I said before was true. She cheated and betrayed me. It put a knife through my heart. I sold everything I owned for the price of a ticket to Africa, where I built water purification systems for villages. I never wanted to see the civilized world again. This job came along and I took it. I thought the pain was gone, if not the memory. I tried to fight it when you mentioned children in Lucerne. But when Missy went on TV – despite the fact that he was a real sleaze – I just lost it.

Michael's head was down. "That's the explanation. It's no excuse."

"And you bought a ticket on this flight – in Club World – just to tell me that?"

"Yes. I can leave."

Passengers were filling the plane, but it was still almost thirty minutes to departure. The flight attendant who had delivered the flowers was nearby, trying to look like she was working.

"So, was on the boat just pretend?"

"I may have been playing a part when we started, but when you almost got hit by the bridge, I found out it was more than that."

"So, it wasn't just about the 'you know?'"

"The 'you know' was great, but you put yourself in a situation that could have been dangerous and did a great job. I've come to respect you, as well."

"Just respect?"

"No. I love you. I found that out soon after I'd left. I just felt too stupid and embarrassed to . . ."

"You destroyed me for two nights and two days."

"I know. I'm sorry. I could say it a thousand times, and it wouldn't be enough. Maybe someday . . ." He started to gather his things.

"What are you doing?"

"I came to apologize. I've done that. I don't want to ruin your flight."

"You're just going to give up the money this cost? And, when you might – and I mean might – get me to accept your apology?"

Eve saw his face brighten. "Really?!"

Eve sat back and toyed with a rose. "I said 'might.' Besides, I've got too good a bargaining position right now to let you get off this airplane and out of my control."

"I love you more than life itself, you don't have to bargain, you can have anything you want."

"You've got a lot of faith that you can deliver anything I want, you know."

"My life, if necessary." Michael got down on one knee and opened a ring box. Inside was the engagement ring she'd worn on the cruise. "I said when I did it for real, I'd be on one knee. Would you make me the happiest man in the world, forgive me, accept this ring – and consider whether you would marry me?"

Eve jumped out of her seat, knocking the flight attendant back and Michael over. She locked her arms around him and kissed him. "Yes. Yes. Of, course I will," she paused with a coy smile, "consider whether I'll marry you." She kissed him again, and the cabin exploded with cheers and applause.

Michael tried to sit up. "Well, in that case, we've got to get off this airplane. I've got a dinner to fix for you."

"But . . ."

"But nothing. Come on."

"Everybody's going to hate us. They have to pull my luggage off. It will take forever."

"I already had it pulled."

"W-H-A-T?!"

"Come on."

Eve grabbed her bag and they ran down the aisle for the exit. "Pretty confident, aren't you, Michael Thomas?"

"Hopeful. Just hopeful."

"Ladies and gentlemen, welcome to British Airways flight 217 to Dulles International Airport. We apologize for the slight delay, but one of our passengers – make that two of our passengers just got engaged to be married." There was the sound of applause and cheers from the back of the plane. "Please make sure your seat belts are securely fastened and your tray tables are up and secured. As a special treat, in honor of the engagement, complimentary champagne will be served during this flight." There were more cheers and applause.

Three seats back from where Eve and Michael were sitting, on the other side of the airplane, John Kelly lowered a newspaper and smiled. He was happy and he knew Meg would be happy. Mostly, they would be happy because Michael and Eve were happy.

A flight attendant passed by John. Four rows back, she handed a glass of champagne to a tall thin man with short dark hair.

"Thank you," he said.

She said, "You're welcome. That's a unique lapel

pin, I've never quite seen one like it before."

The man raised soft gray eyes to meet hers and said, "Really? It's Saint Jude. Patron saint of lost causes. A favorite of mine."

Thirty-seven

Eve Thomas lay naked in bed, eyeing her swollen belly. "You did this to me. And now that I'm getting fat, you won't love me anymore."

Michael rolled toward her. "You are beautiful. You were, you are, you always will be. And, I will love you forever."

"This is your fault, you know. I blame you, even if it did lead to a line of Eve-M maternity clothes."

"Well, our fault, My Love. You helped – and very nicely, I might add."

"I still think you won't love me now that I'm fat. You'll look for somebody else." She said it with a faux pout. But as she said it, Eve realized that the specter of her weight issues was gone – chased out or destroyed by their love. *He will love me no matter what, maybe more now than before. Wasted worries.*

"Eve, there could never be anyone else." He kissed her belly.

"You're not just saying that?"

He kissed her belly again, then worked his way up to her breasts.

Eve giggled. "Take it easy, there. The girls are getting sensitive."

Michael slid his body between her legs, kissed her passionately, and said, "Then, I'll just have to show you in some other way."

Their lips met. Their tongues played. He entered her and she pulled him down.

"I never thought," Eve started.

"I love you more than life itself," he said.

Moving together, slowly, passionately, they both had found heaven.

Thank you for reading my book. I hope you enjoyed it.

If you liked this book, please leave a review. Reviews help other readers find books they would like to read and help authors improve their own works.

In addition, if you would like to be one of my beta reviewers – someone who reads my books before publication and who receives the completed book free of charge, please send your name and e-mail address to my publisher at TWeaver2008@aol.com to be included in this group. You may opt out at any time. You can also contact me through my website https://www.annaleighromance.com/

Books by Anna Leigh

Loves Lost and Found – A Mystery Romance Adventure

Lost in the Forest – A Romantic Wilderness Adventure

River Cruise Undercover – A Romantic Travel Adventure

Coming soon: Rocky Mountain Romance

ABOUT THE AUTHOR

Anna Leigh lives in suburban Maryland. She enjoys musical theater, loves to travel, and cares for small animals. She also enjoys fitness activities and has completed numerous Spartan challenges.

Made in the USA
Middletown, DE
19 October 2020